MARGARET M

THE XENA ISLAND MYSTERY

Complete and Unabridged

LINFORD
Leicester

First published in Great Britain in 2021

First Linford Edition
published 2021

A catalogue record for this book is available from the British Library.

ISBN 978–1–4448–4770–3

Published by
Ulverscroft Limited
Anstey, Leicestershire

Printed and bound in Great Britain by
TJ Books Ltd., Padstow, Cornwall

This book is printed on acid-free paper

THE XENA ISLAND MYSTERY

On the beautiful Mediterranean island of Xena, Zara's peace is shattered by a phone call from her ex-husband Owen. It turns out that, thanks to him ticking the wrong box on the divorce form, they are still very much married! Now engaged to someone else, Owen wants to finalise the divorce properly. Zara is more than happy to oblige. But when he flies out to Xena to meet with her, things become — well, complicated . . .

Startling News

Zara could hear the tide lapping the white sands and the cheerful shouts of surfers breaking the crested waves. The afternoon air was heavy with the mingled scents of oregano and wild thyme. She closed her eyes and counted to ten before taking a firm hold on her mobile.

'What do you mean we are not divorced?' she asked in a careful voice.

'I, um, may have ticked the wrong box on the form.'

Owen sounded like a schoolboy coming up with an excuse for not completing his homework.

'Is this some sort of joke?' Zara's eyes narrowed in suspicion. She would put nothing past her ex-husband or, as she had discovered a few moments ago, the man who was still her husband.

'No, it's for real.'

A group of young surfers strolled past, looking as though they hadn't a care in the world. Until a few moments ago Zara thought her life was also on an even keel.

'Zara, are you still there?'

Zara saw no reason to break the awkward pause and it was Owen who spoke first.

'Sir Robert was most sympathetic to our cause.'

'Who is Sir Robert?' Zara demanded in as controlled a voice as she could manage.

'He was the senior judge at our hearing.'

'Whoa, hold on.' Zara sat bolt upright, her notepad slipping off her knee. 'What hearing?'

'The family court one.'

'Are you saying you held this hearing without me?'

'What else could we do?' Owen sounded as though the whole thing were Zara's fault. 'We couldn't find you and you didn't reply to any of my texts. I didn't even know if I was contacting the right number.'

Zara bit her lip. After her marriage ended she had cut all ties with Owen, changed her mobile number and deleted any mention of him from all her social media accounts. She had also blocked his number.

'How did you find me? I presume you haven't done anything illegal.' Zara experienced a qualm of concern that she instantly quashed.

'Duncan.'

'I might have known he'd break his promise.' Zara sighed.

'He did owe me one, or two — several come to that.'

'So you resorted to blackmail.'

'I wouldn't put it quite like that.' Owen was sounding awkward again.

'I'll take that as a yes.'

'It is an emergency.' He made it sound as though Zara were the unreasonable one.

She took another deep breath. Speaking to Owen resurrected all the old emotions. His voice still sounded the same, sort of gravelly.

She remembered the remote island in the Pacific when he had proposed to her and how they had married six weeks later on a beach in Bali. Their whirlwind courtship was followed by an equally whirlwind marriage. It was over within the year.

Zara had emerged emotionally battered and bruised but not beaten. Never again would she fall for a man with dark brown eyes and sticky-out ears.

'Zara, I know it's my fault and I am sorry, but I'm trying to put things right.'

'Paperwork never was your strong point, was it?' The bitterness of her marriage to Owen had faded after three years. She had moved on and these days it was easier to remember the happy times they had spent together.

'Mossy is most insistent we get things cleared up as soon as we can.'

'Mossy?' Zara dragged her thoughts back to the present. It didn't do to go soft on Owen. He was a Grade A rat.

'My girlfriend — fiancée actually — her real name is Amosede. Hang on, I'll show you a picture.' An image of Amosede pinged on to Zara's screen.

'Isn't she beautiful?'

Zara swallowed. She had to admit Amosede Valentine more than lived up to her description.

'Is she a model?' Zara asked in a voice that let her down. How could anyone look that stunning?

'She was.' Owen's voice was full of pride. 'But now she is studying for a degree in law. She wants to major in human rights. She comes from a small African village that doesn't even have running water. As a child she had to walk miles to the well every day and sometimes the water was contaminated.'

Zara blinked her vision back into focus. Nothing could be more removed from her own childhood. Admittedly it wasn't luxurious but there had always been clean water and enough to eat.

'You're calling, I suppose, because you want the situation cleared up as soon as possible?'

'Sir Robert thought it would be best if I contacted you.'

'And there's me thinking this call was

about reconciliation.'

'Zara, this is serious.'

'You don't have to tell me. Bigamy is not an attractive word.'

'You haven't,' Owen paused, 'married again?'

'As a matter of fact I haven't,' Zara was forced to admit. 'No thanks to you.' She paused. 'So update me on your friend Sir Robert.'

'He's a personal friend of Mossy's,' Owen explained. 'He comes from the neighbouring village to hers and when she arrived in London they went around together for a while. It was through Sir Robert that we learned about . . . ' Owen paused as if uncertain how to continue.

'The status of our marriage.' Zara finished his sentence.

'Yes.'

'I suppose there's no mistake?'

'No.' Owen's voice sounded extra gravelly.

'Then we have a problem.'

'Yes.'

'Do you have a solution?' Zara persisted.

'We need to prove we have lived apart for two years,' Owen explained.

'Not difficult.' Zara retrieved her notepad off the floor. 'Since I haven't seen you for three. Where are you, by the way?'

'In the shower, it's the only place I can get a decent signal.'

'I mean what part of the world.'

'Cornwall.'

If Zara closed her eyes she could still see Owen's white walled cottage perched on the brow of the hill.

She remembered how sunsets used to paint the harbour a deep shade of peach at the end of the day. Zara and Owen had often risen at dawn and walked hand in hand down to the cobblestone quay to see the fishing boats bobbing about on the water.

They would perch on the harbour wall while they waited for the fleet to return with the day's catch, the warmth of Owen's body beside hers warding off the early morning chill.

'Seagull's Rest?'

'That's right.' Owen sounded more cheerful now the worst of his confession was over.

'Where's Mossy now?' she asked.

'In London — studying. I know it's a big ask,' Owen wheedled, 'but could we meet up? I'll pay any expenses.'

Zara clenched her jaw. She had no intention of falling in with Owen's plans. He'd broken her heart when he had been unfaithful and now she wanted him to experience what it was like to have your whole world turned upside down in the space of an afternoon.

''Fraid not,' she informed him.

'You're not going to be difficult, are you?' There was a steely edge to Owen's voice.

'I'm surprised Duncan didn't tell you.'

'Tell me what?'

'I'm out of the country and I can't fly home at the drop of a hat because you messed up our divorce papers.' Zara bit her lip and waited for his next move. It wasn't long in coming.

'You're on Xena, aren't you?'

She felt the hair on the back of her neck rise.

'You won't get to see Mertice Yo,' Owen continued as Zara fought to catch her breath. 'She's a virtual recluse these days.'

'Look, Owen,' Zara found her voice and clenched her fists, 'I'm not coming to Cornwall so if you're so keen to get our divorce finalised . . . ' She decided to call his bluff, confident that Xena Island would be the last place he would want to visit.

'I suggest you fly out here to get your papers signed or whatever it is you want me to do.'

'I'll be with you tomorrow.'

The line went dead.

'You do not look happy,' Stan called over from the bar. 'Is it bad news?'

'Could be better.' Zara summoned up a smile.

'Let me cheer you up with my special of the day. It is time for dinner,' he announced. 'I will bring you a plate of mezédes, all fresh ingredients with some pastries to follow.'

Zara sat on the terrace and watched the sun set while Stan prepared her evening meal. It had to be a horrible coincidence for Owen to choose this week to contact her after years of silence.

Xena — the island of hospitality lived up to its description. Her honeymoon here with Owen had been a magical time, a time she had never wanted to end. The days had been long and full of sun and at night they had shared intimate suppers on the beach listening to the gentle waves wash the soft white sand.

She should never have let Duncan persuade her to take on this commission but Zara figured Owen was no longer a part of her life and it would be safe to return. To discover she was still legally married to Owen had shocked her to the core.

It was Duncan who had been the cause of their introduction. He had also arranged their honeymoon on Xena, staying in a property owned by Mertice

Yo, the world-renowned Asian ballerina.

Zara recalled their days exploring the natural beauty of the island, water skiing and snorkelling, hiring a private boat and taking off wherever the blue waters would take them.

She should have known it wouldn't last. Fairy tales seldom did and Zara vowed she would never again allow a man to exercise control over her emotions, a vow she had no difficulty keeping.

Owen had stolen her heart and she knew she couldn't handle such pain again.

The sound of a child's laughter drew her back to the present. At least Owen could not stay long on the island. As training manager and private pilot of a small aviation school, the summer months were his busiest time and he would need to get back home immediately.

'I have for you,' Stan paused dramatically in the doorway of the taverna, 'olives, pitta bread, stuffed vine leaves, taramasalata and small grilled aubergines, and to follow, a selection of my famous honey pastries.' He placed a jug of fruit juice on the table, his dark eyes curious and sympathetic. 'Enjoy. If you need me you know where I am.'

'Thank you, Stan.'

Zara tore off some of the bread and chewed slowly, enjoying the bitter tang of the olives. Sipping fruit juice she started to feel better and convinced herself seeing Owen again was no big deal, she could handle it and after tomorrow he would be out of her life for ever.

* * *

'I'm off out for a walk,' she called to Stan the next day.

'You are looking better.' His eyes signalled approval. 'See you later.' He smiled. 'The fresh air will do you good.'

Zara paused on the outside steps, her eyes adjusting to the brilliant sunshine while she decided what to do. She needed to fill the hours until Owen arrived. Duncan expected a daily report and working would distract her from the challenges to come.

With these thoughts in mind she decided to see if Mertice Yo was in the mood for visitors. She owed it to Duncan to give this assignment her best shot.

Xena provided an ideal hideaway for travellers who wished to stay out of the public eye. The locals had chosen not to go down the tourist route and its location was a closely guarded secret.

Zara shaded her eyes against the glare of the dazzling sunlight as it reflected off the low stone walls. The ground was dusty under her feet and as she struggled up the hilly path she wished she had thought to wear stouter shoes.

A wild goat pranced past her, bleating to its mate and casting her no more than a cursory glance made its sure-footed and confident way along the rocky terrain.

'Kaliméra,' she greeted a shepherd who smiled and bowed politely, making way for her to pass him on the narrow path.

Why did Mertice have to live in such

an inhospitable place, Zara thought as she took a short break and sheltered under a plane tree, welcoming the cool shade afforded by its overhanging foliage, while she wondered what to do next.

She had nothing positive to tell Duncan. She had been on the island four days now and until she had received Owen's call she had been thinking about returning home.

The high wall and iron railing gates surrounding Mertice's property were guarded by a particularly ferocious dog, Zara had found out to her cost after she had tried to pay a call on the reclusive ballerina.

There had been no sign of a bell or anywhere to leave a message and frustrated Zara had been forced to return to the taverna. It didn't look as though today's mission would be any more successful. The villa was deserted.

Perching on a jutting out rock, Zara retrieved her phone from her shoulder bag and re-read her notes. An ankle injury had cut short the ballerina's career. She had retired from public life and embarked on a relationship with millionaire Iannis Theodorous.

He had died in mysterious circumstances after rumours of a financial scandal and according to the financial press Mertice had inherited his property portfolio, which included the renowned Temple Theodorous complex.

The complex comprised several balconied houses where Zara and Owen had honeymooned. It wasn't much to go on, Zara reflected as she switched off her phone and put it back in her bag.

Media speculation following Iannis's death had eventually died down and Xena had slipped back into its quiet ways. From time to time references to Mertice were made in the press but she never granted interviews, neither did she appear at any celebrity galas. Gradually, interest in her career waned.

'My journalist's instinct tells me there's a story here,' Duncan had informed Zara. 'Get out there and see what you can find.'

There was no arguing with Duncan and Zara did owe him for standing by her when her marriage failed.

Duncan, as Owen's closest friend, had been their best man and she had expected him to side with Owen. Instead he had offered Zara a job as his personal assistant, found her a flat and helped her pick up the pieces of her shattered life.

'Good morning. Would you like some refreshment?' A voice startled Zara out of her reverie.

Standing in front of her was a portly red-faced man, his monk's habit secured by a braided belt looped around his waist.

'Father Anthony,' he introduced himself.

'Zara Lennox.' She shook his warm hand.

Father Anthony gestured to a blossom filled orchard.

'The faint buzzing noise you can hear in the distance is the sound of my bees. I have been updating them on the day's events and I would like to tell them about our sad visitor. Is something troubling you?'

'Is it that obvious?' Zara was surprised by his question.

'I would say a recent disruption to your life has unsettled you.'

'And you would be right.'

'Perhaps I can help.'

'I doubt it very much.'

He settled down beside her and ferreted around in his wicker basket.

'If I cannot offer you pastoral help, I can offer you some mint tea. It is home-made and most refreshing.'

Zara watched as he unpacked two small tulip shaped glasses and a box containing tiny cubes of a local sweetmeat.

'These are delicious,' he explained. 'I try to ration myself to one a day but when one is entertaining it is possible to get away with two — or more,' he added, a merry twinkle in his eye.

'Efcharistó.' Zara chose a pink coloured confection and popped it into her mouth.

'I see you have picked up a few words of our language. Is this your first visit to our island?'

'I was here a few years ago.' Zara kept her explanation brief.

'And why are you here now?'

Zara recognised the question as simple Xenian curiosity.

'I work for a travel writer and he feels the island's history would be of interest to his readers.'

'I see.'

Father Anthony offered Zara a second sweetmeat.

'He thought Mertice Yo might be a good subject for interview.'

'I fear both of you will be disappointed.'

'Have you met Mertice Yo?' Zara asked.

'She is my landlady.'

'Can you tell me anything about her?' Zara's interest quickened, sensing this could be her first real lead.

'I could but I don't feel I should. I am sorry to disappoint you but I have little to do with the modern world. I make a living growing melons, herbs and olives and aiding you with your research would disrupt my tranquillity.'

Feeling she had earned the justifiable rebuke, Zara apologised.

'Where did you learn to speak English?' she added.

The corners of Father Anthony's mouth curved into a generous smile.

'I picked it up along life's journey and now I have told you all about myself are you going to tell me why your eyes are filled with so much sadness?'

'I could,' Zara parodied back at him, 'but I don't feel I should.'

Father Anthony broke into a hearty laugh, startling the woodchats in the tree above them.

'I asked for that, didn't I?' He paused. 'I see you are doing your best not to glance at your very elegant wrist watch. Are you expecting someone to join you? Someone perhaps you do not want to see?'

With a leaden heart Zara glanced down to see the water taxi making steady progress towards the harbour.

'I have to go.' She rose to her feet.

'Please do not let me keep you.'

'Thank you for your hospitality.'

'My pleasure. I hope our paths cross again. Good luck.'

With a cheery wave he set off towards his olive grove, leaving Zara to make her reluctant way down to the landing stage where Owen would be waiting for her.

Too Many Memories

Zara trod carefully over the worn cobblestones of the main street running through the traditional fishing village before starting on the steep descent to the harbour mooring stage.

Having to concentrate on the uneven incline cancelled out the counter-productive practice of thinking about Owen. The sooner the nightmare of her marriage was over the sooner her life could return to normal.

Although he had his back to her, Zara would have recognised him anywhere. He hadn't changed since she had last seen him, taller than average and with a physique to match.

Zara took a few moments out to watch him strike up an animated exchange with some local fisherman, bargaining with them over the purchase of the last of their day's catch.

As if sensing her presence behind him, he turned slowly to face her. His hair was shorter than she remembered and his eyes were ringed with fatigue.

Zara wished she had thought to freshen up before this meeting. Like Owen, she was wearing an old T-shirt and her crops were stained with drops of Father Anthony's mint tea. She could feel grains of sugar on her lips and rubbed the back of her hand over her mouth to wipe away any remaining evidence of the sweetmeats.

'You missed a bit,' Owen walked slowly towards her and before Zara realised his intention he flicked a sugary crumb off her cheek. 'There, that's better. Hi,' he greeted her.

She fought down the urge to be polite and say how pleased she was to see him. Instead she took a step backwards away from his commanding presence. She wasn't the same person who had fallen for his brand of masculine charm four years ago.

She had grown up and learned Owen Jones was not a man to trust.

'Owen,' she acknowledged with a

cool nod.

'Red mullet,' he replied with his familiar lazy smile, holding up his purchase. 'I don't know about you but I am starved — although from the look of you,' his eyes lingered on the tea stains, 'you might have already eaten.'

'Do you have your paperwork to hand?' She refused to rise to his bait. 'That is the reason for this unscheduled visit, isn't it?'

'It's right here.' He held up a battered briefcase, the one he always took flying.

'I would suggest we get on with it without further delay, wouldn't you?'

'Of course.' Owen nodded. 'Shall we do our business down on the quay or somewhere less public?'

'It's this way.' Zara turned on her heel, forcing Owen to fall into step beside her.

'I'm glad you didn't dress up for this meeting,' he said in a conversational tone, 'I arranged everything in a rush, too.'

'Is that why you didn't bother to shave?' Zara countered back at him.

Owen ran a rueful hand over his stubble.

'You noticed? Stopovers were tight. There wasn't time to visit the rest room between flights.' He smiled again. 'But I'm here now and very pleased to see you. Where are you staying?'

'Stan's Taverna.'

'Everywhere looks pretty much the same, doesn't it?' He shaded his eyes against the heat of the sun. 'I suppose Xena hasn't changed much over the centuries.'

'Left here,' Zara indicated the turning.

'You're cross with me, aren't you?' Owen sounded a shade less confident. His voice held a trace of genuine apology. 'I know I shouldn't have put you in this position.'

'No, you shouldn't.'

'I wasn't thinking straight when I filled in the form,' he attempted to explain, 'and I didn't notice my error.'

'It's not fair to me and it's not fair to Mossy. Don't you realise the trouble you could have caused? Getting divorced isn't a game.'

'No, it isn't.'

'I might have wanted to get married again and I would have been guilty of bigamy,' Zara couldn't help adding.

They walked until Owen suddenly broke the silence.

'Has there been anyone in your life?'

If Owen was fishing for information about her relationships, Zara wasn't going to enlighten him.

'Here we are.' She paused by the brightly painted yellow door leading into the courtyard of the taverna.

'Hey,' Stan came rushing out, almost knocking Zara over. 'Wait for me,' he bellowed down to the boatman.

'Sorry . . . ' Ignoring Owen, he hugged Zara to his chest. 'I didn't hurt you, did I?'

'No.' She rubbed her bruised elbow. 'Where are you rushing off to in such a hurry?'

'To the mainland and the taxi will leave without me if I'm not quick about it. I'll be back later. Help yourself to anything you want and put it on the tab.' He kissed her on the cheek.

'Stan?' Owen asked as they watched him dash off towards the harbour.

'Yes.'

'He seems very friendly.'

'He runs the taverna so if you were looking for him to cook your fish for you, you are out of luck.'

Owen followed her through the courtyard to the cool interior of the bar.

'If you show me where the kitchen is I'm sure I can manage.' He put the mullet down on the table and began searching for a plate before placing them in the huge fridge in the corner of the kitchen. 'There, all ready for later.'

Zara blinked in surprise.

'You've learned to cook?'

A smile tugged at the corner of Owen's mouth.

'Mossy insisted.'

'She clearly had better luck in that direction than I ever did,' Zara replied before biting her lip. 'Sorry, that was a cheap remark.'

'It's a valid comment. I suppose we've both changed over the past few years.'

Zara was the first to look away.

'Would you like a drink?' she asked.

'Water would be great. I'd forgotten how tedious the journey from the mainland could be.'

'It's only a ten-minute ride in the water taxi.'

'Make that half an hour. The pilot was fiddling with something mechanical and there was a peculiar smell coming from the engine. At one stage I thought we were going to have to swim for it.'

'So that's the funny smell.' Zara grabbed some filtered water.

'I beg your pardon?'

She wrinkled her nose.

'Oil,' she informed him.

'I can still taste it at the back of my throat. Where's that water?'

'Here you are, straight from the fridge.' Zara picked up her own glass.

'What do we do now?' she asked.

'There's a flight home this evening I'd like to catch so if I could explain things to you?'

'Let's go outside, the veranda overlooks the harbour. You'll be able to see the taxi as it comes in.'

'Perfect. Do you want to sort out a table while I dig out the paperwork?'

Zara sank into one of the wicker chairs and closed her eyes in relief. It was over. After today Owen Jones would be out of her life for ever. She felt it might be time to make a complete break from the past. She could start looking for a new job.

Duncan would always be friendly with Owen and she needed to sever the contact. It wouldn't be easy. Working for Duncan was a dream job. He travelled the world researching locations for documentaries and travel articles and that was how she had met Owen.

Detained in a business meeting and intending to fly over to France later in the evening, Duncan had asked Zara to deliver some urgent paperwork to a small private airfield on the south coast.

Owen had been the duty officer on reception and while they waited for

Duncan they had enjoyed a snack in the airfield cafeteria. Zara had suffered a recent relationship break-up and Owen had proved a sympathetic listener.

'Here we are.' Owen's voice broke into Zara's thoughts. He produced a file and sat down beside her. 'Sorry to be so last-minute about things but with Mossy's schedule it's difficult to pin down a date for our wedding. She has a gap late August, so we're hoping to arrange something maybe early September.'

'Will you honeymoon in Cornwall?' Zara asked, unaware of the dreamy look turning her eyes a deeper shade of blue.

Owen paused from searching through his papers as he took in her expression.

'You were happy there, weren't you?'

'I remember the sunsets were out of this world.'

'You used to like the way your feet sank into the wet sand after the tide went out.'

'Do you remember Jam?'

'The old fisherman you called Jim and I named Sam?'

'So we wound up calling him Jam. I wonder what happened to him?'

Owen's papers lay untouched on the table between them. A faint breeze disturbed the trailing bougainvillea creating a small shower of petals.

'Excuse me.' A disturbance in the doorway made her jump. 'I am sorry to intrude but I was looking for Stan. Ah,' Father Anthony's face lit up, 'this is the visitor you were expecting, is it not? How nice to meet you.' He extended a hand, 'Zara did not tell me your name.'

'Owen Jones.' He stood up as he introduced himself.

Father Anthony subjected him to an intense inspection.

'Hmm,' he said in a non-committal voice as if he wasn't impressed with what he saw.

'Stan's not here.' Zara jumped in with her explanation, worried Father Anthony might be indiscreet. 'I can give him a message,' she offered.

'I've brought some fresh herbs and melons and olives.' Father Anthony paused. 'I saw red mullet in the fridge.'

'I bought them from the fishermen about an hour ago,' Owen said.

Father Anthony beamed.

'It would give me great pleasure to cook supper for you. No,' he held up a hand to quell any protest, 'I enjoy cooking and eating on one's own can get tedious. You don't mind me joining you?'

Lost for words, Zara looked at Owen.

'I haven't interrupted anything, have I?' Father Anthony asked.

'I think it's a splendid idea.' Owen pushed his file away. 'Why don't I sort out some wine.' He hesitated. 'Unless you would prefer something else?'

'I was going to suggest the very same thing. Now, Zara — I may call you Zara?' She nodded. 'And there's no need to be so formal. I am Anthony. Zara, you do the table, we'll sit out here where we can see the water taxi arrive.'

After making a helpless gesture at Owen Zara set about sorting out cutlery and plates.

'I had forgotten it is Stan's day for

going across to the mainland.' Anthony refreshed everyone's glasses.

'I think he had, too,' Owen remarked, 'judging by the way he rushed out of the taverna.'

'It is good though because it means tonight we are his sole guests. We can indulge ourselves without feeling guilty. How is your mullet?'

'Delicious,' Zara replied as she finished the last morsel of her fish.

'Do you have room for some melon?' Anthony asked. 'I know you have a sweet tooth, Zara, but perhaps too much sugar in one day is bad for us. Fresh fruit would be better, I think.' Not waiting for her reply, Anthony bustled away.

'What did he mean about too much sugar?' Owen demanded. 'I get it,' his brow cleared, 'you've been eating sweets with him, haven't you?'

'What's it to do with you if I want to eat sweets with Anthony or have supper with Stan?'

'You didn't tell me about suppers with Stan.' A corner of Owen's mouth curved with amusement. 'What else have you been getting up to on Xena?'

'Raised voices.' Anthony returned with plates of sliced melon. 'A lovers' quarrel?'

'Sorry.' Zara picked up her spoon.

'I hope it's nothing serious,' Anthony said.

'It wasn't anything,' Zara insisted.

'That's good, because you'll have lots of time to make up.'

'Say again?' Owen frowned at Anthony.

'You won't be going home tonight, Owen.'

'What?' Owen dropped his melon spoon.

'I've just heard the news from one of Stan's cousins. The water taxi has suffered a serious mechanical failure and will be out of action for at least two days. Stan is stuck on the mainland.'

Zara gaped at Owen in undisguised belief.

'You'll have to stay over until the problem is fixed.'

'Not if I have anything to do with it.'

Owen pushed back his chair. 'Excuse me, I have to make a telephone call.'

'What is so important it cannot wait two days?' Anthony asked with a mild smile.

'I need to contact my fiancée.'

Owen strode off in search of his mobile.

'Forgive me,' Father Anthony said. 'I jumped to the mistaken conclusion that you and Owen were married.' Anthony's round face was filled with curiosity as he looked at Zara.

'We are,' she admitted in a hollow voice.

'Darling.' Owen's voice floated through from the bar, 'You won't believe what's happened.'

Visitor in the Night

Father Anthony held up a restraining hand.

'I have spoken out of turn. Your relationship with Owen is none of my business. Don't say another word. People overhear gossip and if you reveal more details someone will start spreading rumours.'

'There's no-one else here,' Zara pointed out.

'Don't you have an expression in English about walls having ears?' Anthony looked unusually serious. 'I do not mean to be impolite, Zara, but in my former life I was the subject of gossip and I know how cruel it can be.

'So,' he began clearing the table before Zara had taken his last comment on board, 'I will find Stan's keys. We will lock up the taverna before we make our way up the hill to my modest dwelling.'

'Surely I can stay here overnight,' Zara protested, 'I will be quite safe.'

'You will not,' Anthony corrected her.

'What do you mean?' Zara experienced a tinge of alarm.

'It is a regrettable fact of modern life. When word gets round that Stan is away.' Anthony shrugged. 'Shall we say the young men of the village will be tempted?'

'To do what?'

'To drink him dry,' Anthony replied bluntly.

'I won't let them in.'

'You won't be able to stop them and it has happened before. We have a severe unemployment problem. It grieves me to say it but housebreaking is not an unusual occurrence.'

'Surely someone should sleep over to keep an eye on things.'

'Stan would never forgive me if something happened to you.'

'Owen can stay over with me. He's capable of taking care of himself.'

'We do not know him. You say he is your husband but if anything should go missing, he is the outsider. He will naturally be the first to come under suspicion.'

Zara thought she had understood local philosophy but she was forced to accept the fact human behaviour was the same the world over.

'What are you talking about?' Owen had come back into the bar without Zara noticing.

'Anthony has invited us to spend the night with him,' Zara explained.

'I couldn't impose on your hospitality,' Owen protested.

'You have no choice, my young friend.' Anthony produced a set of keys from under the bar. 'Now if you are ready? Perhaps, Zara, you would like to pack an overnight bag. Owen, I can lend you anything you might need.'

'May I have a private word,' Owen enquired, 'with Zara?'

Anthony pocketed his keys.

'Certainly, I will wait for you and your wife outside.'

'How does Anthony know we are married?' Owen demanded.

'It slipped out.' Zara made a dismissive gesture with her hands. 'Never mind all that — did you get through to Mossy?'

'I did and she's not best pleased.'

'I can imagine,' Zara said.

'What do you mean?'

'You've told her of your enforced stay on Xena, a situation made worse by the presence of your soon to be ex-wife. In her shoes I would probably suspect you of being up to something.'

Owen's lips straightened into a tight line.

'Mossy would not stoop so low. We trust each other.'

Zara flushed at the implied criticism of her behaviour when she found out about Owen and Joanne Moore.

'I trusted you until you betrayed me.'

'Whatever.' Owen shook his head. 'We can't stay over with Anthony.'

'Unless you intend swimming across to the mainland or sleeping al fresco we have no choice and if you remember, the police patrol the beach at night.'

It was Owen's turn to look uncomfortable. In the early days of their honeymoon and after a beach barbecue he and Zara had been lulled asleep by the gentle music of the waves washing the white sand.

An irate official flashing a torch in their eyes and demanding to know what they were up to had rudely awakened them. It had taken all Owen's powers of persuasion to win over the official and assure him they weren't vagrants nor were they up to any mischief.

'Anthony is locking up now.' Zara pushed home her advantage. 'Can't you hear him?'

'Mossy rearranged her schedule in order for us to firm up on the date for our wedding.'

Zara felt Owen's muscles stiffen as she put a hand on his arm to comfort him. There was the sound of keys being turned in locks and shutters being lowered.

'You always told me to adapt to circumstances and see what developed.'

Owen's eyelids flickered briefly before he gave a curt nod of acknowledgement. 'I suppose there is nothing we can do about the situation. I'll fetch my briefcase from the veranda and see you outside.'

He shook Zara's hand off his arm. With her heart thumping in her chest, Zara headed up to her room and crammed a few essentials into an overnight bag before grabbing her valuables from the small safe.

As she ran downstairs she realised to her dismay she had mislaid the document Owen had asked her to sign before Father Anthony had arrived and disrupted their plans for the evening. She hoped Owen had scooped it up with the rest of his paperwork and put it in his briefcase.

'Is everyone ready?' Anthony asked. 'Then follow me.'

The light was fading from the day as they trudged up the hill, each lost in their own thoughts.

'Here we are.' Anthony paused in front of a low walled one-storey whitewashed building. 'I will do my best to make you comfortable.'

Zara was surprised to discover how clean and luxurious it was inside, far removed from the modest accommodation she had been expecting. The furniture was modern contemporary and Anthony even had a huge flat-screen television fixed on a far wall.

'One of my weaknesses is watching football,' he confessed with a shamefaced smile.

Zara sniffed, sure she could detect a faint aroma of roses. It reminded her of an exclusive French perfume Duncan had brought her one birthday when she was feeling low after her break up with Owen.

Anthony flicked a switch, bathing the kitchen in harsh electric light.

'Would anyone like any more refreshment tonight?'

'No, thank you,' Owen answered for them both.

'Then I will show you where you can freshen up. Owen, I am sure you would like to soak in a hot tub and Zara I have a room with an en-suite shower for you.'

Relieved to discover Anthony had not put her and Owen in a double room Zara said goodnight and closed her bedroom door firmly behind her. She heard the sound of retreating footsteps on the stone flooring outside as the two men walked off down the corridor.

Breathing a sigh of relief, Zara headed for the shower. Again the fixtures and fittings were state of the art. She had not expected Anthony to offer such luxurious guest facilities. The small bathroom was equipped with every need — fluffy towels, soap, shampoo, shower gels, even a toothpaste and brush.

Too tired to give the matter further thought, Zara stood under the powerful jet of water. After towelling herself dry, she slipped under the cool cotton sheets, closed her eyes and fell asleep.

She awoke with a start. It was dark outside but something had disturbed her sleep. Attuning her ears she recognised the sound as the low murmur of voices. One she could identify as Anthony, the other was lighter and more clipped and could have been female.

Pushing back her sheets, Zara swung her feet over the side of the bed. Her investigative instinct was telling her Anthony was not all he seemed.

He purported to be a recluse yet he lived in a small luxury dwelling furnished in the latest style and he had mentioned in the past being hounded by gossip-mongers.

Zara padded to the door, pausing before she opened it. She hesitated as she considered her next move. Owen was sleeping in a room further down the corridor and she had no wish to bump into him in her pyjamas. Common sense kicked in. She decided whatever Anthony was doing was none of her business. She was a guest in his house and he made the rules.

With a puzzled sigh she returned to her bed and switching out the light fell back to sleep.

* * *

A gentle knock on her door stirred her from her slumbers.

'Breakfast is ready.' She heard Owen's voice outside.

Zara jumped out of bed and into the shower. Today would be the day she would sign the papers formally ending her marriage to Owen Jones and she needed to be in a positive frame of mind.

Dressing in a white T-shirt and clean casual shorts she opened the door to her room. There was no-one on the terrace but breakfast had been laid out for her and Owen.

Zara peered over the balustrade overlooking the drive leading down to the village.

What she saw convinced her she had not been imagining things. Anthony had had a night-time visitor — a visitor whom she suspected liked to wear French perfume.

More Than Meets the Eye

'There you are.' Zara spun round at the sound of Owen's voice. 'I was beginning to think you didn't want to get up. Anthony's gone off somewhere so it's just you and me for breakfast. There's fresh yoghurt, figs and honey, orange juice and a huge pot of coffee.'

'Tyre tracks,' Zara replied in an expressionless voice.

'What was that?' Owen's hand stalled over the coffee pot.

'On the road, there, look.' She indicated to where the ground had recently been disturbed. Owen glanced in the direction of her pointing finger. 'Anthony had a visitor in the night. I heard them talking.'

'This is his house. He is entitled to visitors.'

'In the small hours?'

'And you suspect him of doing what in the small hours?' Owen teased. 'Gun running? People smuggling? Heading up a crime syndicate?'

'I don't know.' Zara grew impatient with herself. In the cold light of day her suspicions did seem far-fetched.

Owen poured out the coffee.

'Here, drink some of this. It might help you get your head together.'

'Owen, something's not right.'

He put down the coffee pot with a sigh.

'If Anthony is up to something,' he spoke in a logical voice, 'why did he insist we spent the night here?'

'Perhaps he needed an alibi.'

'Why?'

'I don't know. I'm thinking off the top of my head.'

'You're overreacting.' A superior smile played on Owen's lips. 'Have some of this honey, it's delicious.'

Zara shook out one of the cream linen serviettes provided and held it up for inspection.

'Look at this.'

'What's bugging you now?' The trace of amusement in Owen's voice deepened.

'Laundry not up to your exacting standards?'

'Don't you find all this strange?' She indicated their surroundings. 'Laundered serviettes, fluffy bath towels, toiletries? It doesn't go with the image of a man of simple means.'

'What are you implying?' Owen paused from spooning up a mouthful of yoghurt.

'It's Anthony.' Zara screwed up her face. 'He's all wrong.'

'You've been reading too many spy thrillers,' Owen chided.

'And have you smelled perfume?'

'Now you are delving into the realms of fantasy.'

'I'm not,' Zara insisted. 'Why won't you take me seriously?'

'Look.' Owen softened the expression on his face. 'Even if Anthony is up to something it's no business of ours.' He shook Zara's hand. 'Is it?'

'I suppose you're right,' Zara was forced to admit.

'What you should be concentrating

on is asking Anthony to help you get an introduction to Mertice Yo. I believe she is his landlady?'

'Yes.'

'A word of advice.' Owen tapped the side of his nose. 'Accusing him of gun running is not the way to go about it.' 'I never said he was doing anything illegal.' Zara began to tighten up again.

'Not in so many words.'

'Shall we drop the subject?' Zara sensed the exchange might take an unpleasant turn if they carried on in the same vein.

'Good idea.'

For a few moments they ate in silence before Zara spoke.

'You know why I am here but why are you here?'

'Come again?' Owen looked baffled.

'The divorce thing isn't just a cover?'

'I don't follow.'

'This is one of your busiest times of the year.'

'Agreed, but I do have good back up staff.'

'You should be moving mountains to

get home.'

'Go on.' Owen was looking intently at Zara.

'You're not using our divorce as an excuse to looking into the possibility of developing this peaceful island by landing tourist-laden gas-guzzling aircraft here, are you?'

'I'm not sure I understood you correctly.' Owen spoke carefully.

Zara frowned.

'What I'm trying to say is, are you on the make?'

With an angry gesture, Owen threw down his starched serviette.

'I know my arrival has stressed you but I promise I have no hidden commercial agenda. You can rest easy. I love Xena as it is and I hope to bring Mossy here one day. I also plan to leave the island as soon as the water taxi is operational. Have I set your mind at rest?'

Zara squirmed, knowing she was in the wrong but reluctant to admit it.

'Why did the water taxi have to choose now to suffer mechanical failure?' She ran a hand through her hair.

'I don't know but it was nothing to do with me and if I put my mind to it I may be able to hitch a lift from a passing fisherman.

'However, if I can't, an extra day would give us time to finalise our situation and make sure we haven't made any more mistakes.'

'I didn't make any in the first place.'

'To make sure I haven't made any more mistakes, then.

'Now have we cleared the air between us? I want us to be friends.'

Zara grimaced as she sipped more coffee. Owen picked up on her shudder.

'It is a bit strong, isn't it? Have some yoghurt, help wash it down.'

'Owen . . .' She bit her lip, uncertain how to go on.

'What's really worrying you?' he asked.

Anthony bustled on to the terrace looking far from refreshed after his night's sleep.

'Good morning, Zara, I am sorry I was not here to greet you before breakfast. Is there enough for another cup?' He eyed up the coffee pot.

Zara greeted his arrival with a sense of relief. She hadn't relished telling Owen his journey might have been a monumental waste of time because she had lost his wretched form.

Anthony cut into a ripe fig, quartering it before popping a segment into his mouth.

'I am sorry to be the bearer of bad news, Owen.' Owen waited patiently for him to continue. 'Stan's cousin informs me the water taxi will be out of action for another twenty-four hours. I hope the delay will not inconvenience you too much.'

'Could someone ferry me across to the mainland? I'm willing to pay.'

'Could you not wait one more day? Your time will not be wasted. I need help in the olive grove. We could have a picnic lunch and perhaps take a stroll up to Mertice's villa later?'

'We can't keep imposing on your hospitality.'

'Nonsense. I don't mind at all. Zara?' Anthony raised his eyebrows. 'What do you think?'

Zara hesitated, unable to come up with a suitably polite excuse.

'I think Zara would be pleased if you helped her gain an interview with Mertice,' Owen admitted.

'I can speak for myself, thank you,' she interjected.

'You need to do your research,' Anthony appeared not to hear her remark, 'and I have provided you with a perfect opportunity. After lunch we could take a little walk and I could tell you something about the local area, fill in some gaps for you?'

'That's a kind offer but I didn't bring my laptop with me. It's still at the taverna.'

'You won't need it. Besides, Stan has not returned so it is still closed up.'

'You have the keys, don't you?' Owen said. 'You could let us in.'

'I don't think so,' Anthony replied in a dismissive voice signifying the matter was not up for discussion. 'Why don't you clear the table while I prepare the picnic?'

'What do we do?' Zara hissed at Owen as Anthony picked up the coffee pot and disappeared in the direction of the kitchen, 'He's locked us out of the taverna.'

'There's nothing we can do.'

'I don't believe I'm hearing this.'

'Zara, it's a setback but nothing we can't handle. How about we take up Anthony's offer of a day in the sunshine?'

'You were the one who was all for leaving a moment ago. Can't you see we're being manipulated?'

'We're not back on that again, are we?'

'I think Anthony wants to keep an eye on us and this water taxi thing has played right into his hands.'

'Let's use the situation to our advantage. It's a beautiful morning and he's offering us some down time. I'm prepared to take him up on his offer. How about you?'

'I am here to work, not to prune olive

trees.'

'If Anthony wants help in the olive grove don't you think we ought to show willing? If I can't get back to the mainland I'll be sitting around kicking my heels so I might as well make myself useful and the same goes for you.'

'I suppose you're right.' Zara conceded defeat, accepting her suspicions could be the result of an over active imagination.

Ever since Owen had arrived she had found it difficult to concentrate on her job and Anthony could prove a fruitful contact.

'Zara heard a disturbance in the night,' Owen announced as the they started off in the direction of the olive grove.

'Indeed?' The expression on Anthony's face gave nothing away. 'What sort of disturbance?'

Zara cast Owen a thunderous look.

'I thought I heard voices.'

'Sleeping in a strange bed after a somewhat disturbed evening, the mind can play funny tricks. What you heard might have been the wind in the pine trees.

‘Now why don’t we place the picnic here in the shade of the wall while we set about our morning’s work?’ Anthony handed out small cutters to both of them. ‘Remove anything overgrown or dead.’

‘We wouldn’t want to damage the shoots,’ Owen said.

‘If you treat my vines kindly they are very forgiving. You know the goddess Athena was reputed to be the first to plant olives in the Mediterranean and the olive is a symbol of peace?’

As they worked the vines Anthony regaled them with the myths and legends associated with the production of vines and some of their history and why they were so revered in the culture of his country.

‘Midday,’ Anthony announced to the sound of a gun going off in the distance. ‘Many of the fishermen do not carry time pieces so the gun is the signal for everyone to take a rest. Come along. It is the local custom to break at midday.’

Anthony led Zara and Owen back to where he had left their picnic basket in the shade.

'Today we have a refreshing cucumber dip, stuffed aubergine, tomatoes, herbs and onions, all home grown, together with local feta cheese and of course some of my own currant bread.

'It is time to relax and enjoy two of my greatest pleasures, food and good company.' He poured out three glasses of mint tea and passed them round. 'I think this is my favourite hour of the day.'

'Is midday a significant time?' Zara paused, wanting to choose her words carefully. 'For meditation?'

'It can be,' Anthony agreed, 'but working on the land it is difficult to choose a time for private contemplation. As I am not part of a sect I set my own disciplines. I have always been independent. It suits my character. Owen, you are looking disturbed. Is something wrong?'

'Someone's approaching,' he said.

A thin bespectacled male in khaki shorts and carrying a backpack was trudging towards them.

'I am sorry to disturb your lunch,' he

began in English with a nervous smile.

'This is private property.' Anthony sounded less friendly.

'I didn't mean to trespass.'

'But you are.' In his agitation Anthony knocked over his glass of mint tea. 'Be off with you and stop bothering us.'

Zara gaped open-mouthed as Anthony shook his fist at the young man who stepped back in alarm. Owen retrieved Anthony's glass from the ground and made a gesture to Zara to remain silent.

'My name is Ned Tripp,' Ned began.

'I said go away.'

'Please.' Ned stood his ground. 'I'm not here to make trouble.'

'Everyone leave.' Anthony was now seriously agitated, leaping to his feet and stuffing their uneaten picnic back into the basket.

'Zara and Owen, thank you for your help. I won't be working in the olive grove this afternoon. I forgot I have something urgent I need to attend to.'

'But Anthony . . . ' Zara became concerned as his breathing grew laboured.

'Couldn't we at least help you carry everything back?'

'I can manage,' he insisted.

He threw away the remains of his mint tea and crammed the cups back into his basket.

'Best do as he says,' Owen murmured in her ear.

'He doesn't look well,' Zara protested.

'We'll probably make matters worse if we hang around. We'll collect our things and be on our way,' he called over to Anthony who did not respond.

Shrugging at Zara, Owen set off leaving a mystified Zara to trundle after him.

Confession Time

'What do we do now?' A dejected Zara clutched her overnight bag.

'Where did that character Ned get to?' Owen looked up the deserted path.

'I have no idea.'

'What did you make of him?'

Zara wished she had thought to tie back her hair. She massaged the base of her neck with the palm of her hand but it brought little relief from the intense heat of the sun.

'Like everything else in this affair, it doesn't make sense.'

'Agreed,' Owen conceded.

'Do you think Anthony's unwell? I mean he changed character before our eyes.'

'I don't think he's suffering dual personality issues but something spooked him. I wonder where Ned hangs out.'

'He probably took off after Anthony's outburst and I don't blame him.'

'We'd better move it, too, in case

Anthony follows us. There's no knowing what he might do.'

'Stop pushing me,' Zara objected as Owen delivered a sharp nudge in her ribs.

'Then get going,' he urged.

'Are you sure we're doing the right thing?' Zara hesitated. 'You saw Anthony up there — he's ill. We can't walk out on him.'

'What do you suggest we do?'

'I'm thinking things through.'

'Don't take too long about it.'

'I want to know what's going on.' Zara's eyes flashed. 'You can go if you like but I'm not running away like a scalded cat.'

'Anthony is a grown man, Zara. He doesn't need us to run his life.'

'That's it.'

'What is?'

'His life.'

'Now what are you talking about?'

'He mentioned something about being the subject of gossip in his former life.'

'Your point is?'

'Do you think Ned is an undercover

reporter?'

'Ned Tripp is no-one's idea of paparazzo.'

'Maybe he's not but something triggered Anthony back there.'

'We can't go back to the taverna. It's locked up and Anthony has the spare key. We could try camping on the beach,' Owen said with a hint of mockery.

'Hey!' A voice further down the hill startled both of them.

'What now?' Owen muttered.

'You are the English couple staying at the taverna?'

'Yes, we are,' Zara confirmed.

'I am Stan's cousin, Darius. I have been looking for you everywhere.'

'We've been staying with Father Anthony,' Owen explained.

The expression on Darius's face suggested rather them than him.

'Stan has texted me to apologise on his behalf. He says he will return to Xena as soon as he can but meanwhile you are to make yourselves as comfortable as possible at his expense.'

'We'll pay our way,' Zara insisted.

'The problem is,' Owen butted in, 'the taverna is locked up.'

'I have a key,' Darius replied.

'Thank goodness.' Zara expelled a long breath of relief.

Darius fell into step beside Zara.

'You had visions of spending a night under the stars?' Darius flashed Zara a smile.

'No.'

'Yes,' Owen contradicted.

'It can be very romantic. You are here on a second honeymoon? How long have you been married?'

'Can we please talk about something else?' Zara pleaded.

'My wife and I have been married six years and we have three little ones,' Darius announced with a proud smile. 'Do you have family?'

Zara threw Owen an exasperated glance.

'We haven't been blessed,' he replied, his expression giving nothing away.

'Don't leave it too long,' Darius

advised, 'Your life changes once you have children and for the better. Now please let yourselves in.' He produced his key.

'I have been neglecting my other duties while I was looking for you. If you need me I live in one of the fishermen's cottages down by the harbour. Ask anyone. They will know where to find me.'

'That was sticky,' Zara said, watching Darius make off in the direction of the harbour. 'He thought we were married.'

'We are, aren't we?' Owen turned the key.

'You know what I mean.'

'And we don't want to upset the locals. They might not like the idea of us staying together in the taverna if our relationship isn't official.'

'We won't be staying together.' Zara was firm.

'For the moment let's do as Darius says,' Owen replied. 'We can have a re-think later.'

'What about?'

'I don't know,' he admitted, 'but we do need to talk and we both need to freshen up. I'll fix myself up with a room and see you on the veranda in half an hour?'

Sitting on the terrace, clutching glasses of cold water, Owen turned to Zara.

'Run it past me again. Why did Duncan send you out to Xena?'

'He wanted a report on the island and, if possible, Mertice Yo. He's thinking about doing a documentary.'

'And so far you have been unsuccessful in getting an interview with Mertice?'

'I didn't hold out much hope in the first place. I know she was close to the disgraced financier Iannis Theodorous and I thought maybe she could tell me something about him.'

'Do you know anything about Mertice Yo?' Owen asked.

'She was a leading ballerina and performed with all the major opera houses before she retired after injuring her ankle in a fall.'

'That's the story I got,' Owen agreed. 'What was Iannis accused of?'

'Fraud — one of those get rich schemes which didn't go as planned. He was still being investigated at the time of his death.'

'Leaving a lot of people very unhappy.'

'If he hadn't died when he did he would probably be behind bars now.'

'No wonder Mertice is a recluse.'

'I wonder how Anthony pays his rent.'

'You don't think Mertice was his mid-night visitor, do you?'

'Why would they meet under cover of darkness?'

'I don't know but I am convinced there was someone in the house last night besides us. You saw the tyre tracks.'

'They could have been made any time.'

'They were fresh. The ground is so hard here from lack of rain that sort of thing doesn't last long.'

'When did you develop detective skills?' Owen asked.

'I've developed a lot of skills since we split up.'

Owen looked away from her as if lost in thoughts of his own.

'Anyway I think I'm going to have to call time,' Zara said. 'My sole lead to

Mertice was Anthony and it looks like he's a spent force so if Duncan wants to pursue the project he'll have to employ someone more professional to do the research.'

'You and Duncan have grown close, haven't you?' Owen gave Zara a searching look.

Zara stiffened, quelling a natural reaction to say they were just good friends. Perhaps it would do Owen no harm if she bigged up her relationship with Duncan. If Owen thought she was still pining after him it was time to disillusion him.

'We have talked about,' Zara said carefully, 'our situation.'

'You're moving in together?'

'I didn't say that,' Zara backtracked. One telephone call between Duncan and Owen would be enough for her ex-husband to work out she was being seriously economical with the truth.

'Anyway, talking of personal relationships, don't you think you should contact Mossy again? She must be dying to know what is going on.'

'You're right, I should. Do you have those papers I asked you to sign?'

Zara's heart plummeted.

'Slight problem,' she admitted.

'Yes?' Owen's voice was as cold as the water in her glass.

'The thing is,' she confessed, 'what with all that has been going on, I'm not sure where they are.'

'You've lost them?'

'I'm sure they've only been misplaced. Have you searched through your brief-case? They could be there.'

'They aren't.'

'How do you know?' 'I gave them to you.' 'I don't know where they are.' 'How could you be so incompetent? Is this a pathetic attempt to get revenge on me?' Anger flared in Zara's eyes. 'I don't know what you're talking about.' 'If you don't sign those papers we are still legally married. Is that what you want?' 'It's the last thing in the world I want.' 'It doesn't seem like it to me.' 'Until a few days ago I thought we were divorced. It was you who got it wrong, not me and if you recall you also said had I married again in the mistaken belief we were divorced I would have been guilty of bigamy.'

'Well, that's not going to happen.'

'What do you mean by that remark?'

'Anyone wanting to marry you has to have serious stability issues.' Zara could no longer restrain her anger. 'You married me and that explains a lot about your state of mind!'

Slamming her glass of water down on the table she swept off the veranda and into the cool interior of the taverna.

'What made you act in such a foolish manner, Anthony?' The forehead of the slim woman sitting opposite him at the pine kitchen table was creased in a displeased frown.

'I panicked,' Anthony admitted.

'You overreacted,' she corrected him, 'Who was this person?'

'He came from nowhere.'

'And you have no idea who he was?'

'I am not sure.'

'Please, I need more than that.'

'He looked vaguely familiar.' Anthony crumpled as he confessed. 'He said his name was Ned Tripp.'

Mertice turned pale.

'Did he recognise you?'

Anthony shook his head an uncertain expression on his face.

'I don't think so.'

'Describe him.'

'Late thirties, early forties, pale skinned. I couldn't see his eyes clearly because he was wearing horn rimmed spectacles but I think they were blue.'

The woman shivered.

'It could be him and if it is then we are not safe.'

'You have no need to be scared, Mertice.' Anthony recovered his composure. He leaned across the table and patted her hand in a gesture of comfort, 'We have alarms and cameras hidden in the trees.'

'Even a state-of-the-art security system isn't going to deter anyone who is intent on breaking in.'

'I have a direct line linked to your close circuit television and don't forget Drosselmeyer. He's an excellent guard dog.'

'He's very good at barking but his skills have never been seriously tested. I doubt he'd pass with flying colours.'

'I shouldn't have stirred things up with my overreaction.' The look of uncertainty was back on Anthony's face. 'I apologise.'

'It's too late for that now. Where do you think this Ned went?'

'I hope I scared him off.'

'But the water taxi isn't back in action yet, is it?'

'No.'

'He could still be on the island.'

'It's possible.'

'What about Zara and Owen?' Mertice changed her line of questioning.

'What about them?'

'Where did they go?'

'They left, too.'

'What were you thinking of?' Mertice wrung her hands.

'You know how bad things were after Iannis died and why we did what we did.' He cast Mertice another worried glance.

'I don't doubt you acted in our best interests but if Zara and Owen's suspicions were not alerted earlier they will be now.'

'What could they possibly be suspicious about? They know you are my landlady but nothing else.'

'Which makes your behaviour all the more inexplicable. They will be curious, and what happens if they bump into Ned

Tripp and start talking?'

'I'm fresh out of ideas,' Anthony admitted.

Mertice patted a strand of dark hair back into her bun, a nervous gesture of hers. Although she had not danced for many years she still kept her hair neatly pinned back away from her face and she liked to check everything was in place.

'Well, we shall have to wait and see what happens and one thing we are good at is waiting. Why did you invite Zara and Owen up here in the first place?'

'I wanted to find out how much they knew about your circumstances.'

'And did you?'

'I couldn't ask too many questions because Zara heard us talking.'

'When was this?'

'During the night. I know because she asked if I'd had a visitor.'

'This gets worse.'

'I don't think she was totally convinced by my explanation.'

'What did you tell her?'

'I said it was the wind in the pine trees,

something along those lines.'

'You're right. It is not convincing but there is nothing we can do about things now.'

'I suppose not.'

'You know their first visit to the island was so romantic.' Mertice's dark brown eyes softened at the memory.

'Whose first trip are you talking about?'

'Owen's and Zara's. They went for long walks and picnics and would be gone for hours.' Mertice's rosebud lips curved into a smile.

'I was worried when the police brought them back to the complex one night, but it turned out all they were guilty of was falling asleep on the beach.

'I had to peer through my shutters because I didn't want to be seen. Flashing blue lights and officials in uniform bring back memories I would rather kept hidden.'

'It has to be like this,' Anthony reminded her in a gentle voice.

'Sometimes I long to tell everyone the truth.'

'The world thinks you are a recluse, Mertice, which is how things must stay.'

'But for how long?'

'As long as it takes.'

'Do you think I should talk to Zara?'

'That is the one thing you must not do.'

'She didn't look the type of girl who would be put off by Drosselmeyer.' Mertice fondled the dog's ears.

As if to prove her point Drosselmeyer gave a gentle woof.

'You saw Zara?' Anthony demanded.

'I caught sight of her image on the security camera. She was peering through the railings and when she showed no sign of going away I let Drosselmeyer out to stretch his legs and it did the trick. When next I looked out she had disappeared.' Mertice closed her eyes.

'All this anxiety is stressing me out. Put some music on, Anthony. Tchaikovsky always soothes my nerves.'

Moments later the strains of the 'Swan Lake' overture filled the small kitchen.

Mertice leaned back with a satisfied

smile on her face.

'Dancing the part of the swan princess was such a demanding role but so satisfying.'

'You were wonderful, my darling.' Anthony's weather-beaten faced was wreathed in smiles as together they relived the memory of Mertice Yo's glittering career.

'I had royalty and world leaders falling at my feet. Life was a dream in those days. How did we get into this mess?' Mertice raised her finely plucked eyebrows, a look of intense sadness on her face.

'Thank goodness we have each other.'

Mertice squeezed Anthony's hand as the overture came to an end. The ensuing silence brought with it a return to reality.

'What is this?' Mertice glanced at the sheets of paper scattered on the table between them.

'I found them on the floor of the taverna when we were closing up. I meant to give them back to Owen but when I read their content I decided to hold on to them.'

'You read private papers belonging to someone else?'

'Not intentionally. I wasn't wearing my glasses and first of all I mistook them for my own notes. When I realised what I was reading it was too late.'

'Why are you so vain? Wearing glasses is not a sign of weakness.'

'My vanity may work to our advantage.' Anthony leaned forward full of enthusiasm, 'They are divorce papers.'

'What?' Mertice put a horrified hand to her mouth. 'Whose?'

'Owen and Zara's.'

'No!' She looked as though she were about to burst into tears. 'It cannot be.'

'It is, I am afraid.'

'They were perfect together. My heart is broken.'

She put a hand to her chest, the suggestion of tears in her eyes.

'Never mind your broken heart.' Anthony flapped his hands. 'Don't you see what this means?'

'Two young people have fallen out of love.'

'Concentrate,' Anthony insisted.

'I want no more talk of divorce. You must give those papers back. It will give you a chance to apologise for your earlier rudeness and if you could persuade them to get back together?'

'Don't talk nonsense,' Anthony chided. 'Now pay attention, Mertice. When they realise the papers are missing they will need duplicates which will mean leaving the island to get them.'

Mertice shook her head, still looking distressed.

'How did they fall out of love?'

'Will you stop going on about love?' Anthony looked annoyed. 'As soon as the water taxi is back in action they will be off the island and the threat of discovery will be over and our life can revert to normal.'

'You call this normal? Hiding behind a shutter every time someone visits?'

'Don't overexcite yourself.'

'I can feel one of my headaches coming

on. Where is my cologne?' Mertice gestured towards the dresser. 'I left it over there.'

Anthony picked up the bottle and a delicate lace handkerchief embroidered with Mertice's initials.

'You are not to worry about a thing,' he insisted.

'I can't help it. Visitors unsettle me.'

'Have you had any other visitors recently?'

'I don't think so.' Mertice pressed her lace handkerchief to her brow.

'You don't think so?' Anthony frowned.

'I wasn't going to tell you.' A worried expression crossed the fine features of her face. 'I know how anxious you get.'

'Tell me what?'

'In the shower a few days ago I thought I heard something.'

'What sort of something?'

'I could have imagined it,' Mertice prevaricated.

Drosselmeyer stiffened and growled at the door.

'What is it, boy?' Anthony asked.

The dog let out a loud bark. Mertice clutched her throat dramatically.

'There's someone outside.'

'Leave this to me.'

'No!' Mertice grabbed out at the sleeve of his robe. 'Remember your heart condition.'

'I have every right to protect our property.'

'You might get injured.'

Anthony peered through the blinds.

'Can you see anything?' Mertice whispered.

'There's a shadow down by the gate.'

Drosselmeyer was now scratching frantically at the door.

'Don't go outside. It's not safe.'

'I have to.'

Gesturing at Mertice to stay where she was Anthony unlocked the door and peered out into the garden. Drosselmeyer pushed past him and barking madly hared off down the drive.

Nightmare Situation

'I have good news, Zara,' Darius announced in his heavily accented English, 'the water taxi is well again. Stan texted me. He will be home tomorrow morning.'

'Thank you, Darius. Have you seen Owen anywhere?' Zara cast an anxious look over her shoulder.

'He go out earlier. I don't know where.'

'Not to worry.' Zara hadn't been looking forward to apologising to Owen for her earlier outburst. Although it was a poor excuse, tension had been building up inside her all day and he had been the target of her release mechanism.

'I will bring you some dinner,' Darius said.

'That won't be necessary,' Zara insisted.

'It is,' Darius contradicted her. 'You are my cousin's guest. He is not here. I take his place. My wife will be insulted if you do not enjoy her cooking. I bring it in from next door. We eat together?'

'I wouldn't want to take you away from your family.'

'My mother-in-law is staying,' Darius confided, the heavy look in his eyes speaking volumes.

Zara smiled understandingly.

'I see. Dinner on the terrace would be perfect.'

'Here.' Darius poured out a glass of white wine. 'A little something for you to drink while you enjoy the sunset. I will not be long.'

Clutching her drink Zara sauntered on to the tiny terrace. She could understand it if Owen had taken himself off somewhere far away from her. She hadn't meant what she had said about stability issues and she felt ashamed of herself. Also she wasn't too sure how she was going to apologise. She didn't want their final parting to be on bad terms.

Down on the quayside the nightlife was hotting up. The sound of voices and laughter drifted across from one of the bars and the smell of grilled fish made

Zara's stomach rumble. Their picnic lunch, such as it was, had been hours ago.

Zara remembered eating no more than a mouthful of one of Anthony's exquisite pastries before the situation exploded.

She rocked gently backwards and forwards on the swing seat, careful not to knock over the colourful vase of spring flowers on the small table in front of her.

Overall, this trip had not been a success. Wherever she went she had been reminded of her honeymoon. She thought she had buried her demons but there was no getting away from them on Xena.

The stark silhouette of the Temple Theodorous further along the coast stood as a constant reminder of the past. Originally called the Temple of Sun, it had been renamed in honour of the financier in acknowledgement of the money he had ploughed into the local economy and before his spectacular fall from grace.

Over the centuries the temple had

been a lookout for invaders from the mainland. These days its role was more a tourist attraction but to Zara it was a blot on the landscape, a harsh memory of what she had thought was the happiest time of her life.

She bit her lip, remembering the night Joanna Moore had confessed to Zara about her affair with Owen. Zara wouldn't have believed her if it hadn't been for Joanna's sister backing her up. The two sisters never agreed about anything but Lucy's corroboration of the story convinced Zara Joanna was telling the truth. When she had confronted Owen he hadn't denied the accusation and in that moment Zara knew her marriage was over.

A small sigh escaped her lips. This nightmare situation would not have happened if Owen had filled in the correct paperwork. Duncan would probably have chosen an appropriate moment to break the news of Owen's re-marriage and that would have been that.

Zara hoped with all her heart Mossy

Valentine would fare better as Owen's second wife.

'You like vegetarian moussaka?' Darius returned with a steaming casserole dish, 'My wife makes it to her own special recipe.'

Zara inhaled the piquant aroma of baked aubergine, courgettes and tomatoes.

'Your wife is an excellent cook.'

With a flourish Darius unfurled a red and white checked tablecloth and doled out two generous portions of moussaka on to plain white plates.

'I hope you are hungry because we have to finish every morsel,' Darius instructed Zara. 'My mother-in-law does not like waste.'

'I thought you said this was your wife's recipe.'

Darius pulled a face.

'She learned it from her mother. I love my mother-in-law Irina to bits but my wife is her only daughter and she still likes to interfere. You understand?'

'With loving kindness, I'm sure,' Zara

started to feel more like her old self with some warm food inside her.

'Of course.'

They ate in companionable silence for a few moments, then she heard approaching footsteps.

'Customers, I think.' Darius pushed away his empty plate.

'It's only me.' Father Anthony poked his head around the door.

Zara looked up, uncertain how to greet him.

'I've brought some freshly picked herbs for you, Darius.'

'Thank you. I will put them away right now.'

'And I will keep Zara company because I am sure you have things to do. I hope you don't mind but on the way in I helped myself to a glass of Stan's excellent wine.'

'You are always welcome here, Anthony. Please,' he indicated the seat he had vacated, 'I need to get back to my family.'

'Thank your wife for me,' Zara called

after him, 'And your mother-in-law.'

Anthony placed his wine on the checked tablecloth before sitting down.

'I owe you an apology.' He spoke slowly. 'You and Owen.' He looked around. 'He is not here?'

'He had to go out,' Zara replied.

'What a pity. My earlier outburst was inexcusable. Strangers make me feel jumpy and when they start asking questions about Mertice . . . ' he paused. 'I do not like it.'

Zara swallowed the urge to contradict Anthony. She had been a stranger to him, a stranger who had been asking about Mertice, but he had trusted her and Owen enough to invite them to sleep over but she decided not to make an issue of it.

Apologies seemed to be the order of the day and she was hardly in a position to take offence when her own behaviour had been as bad.

'Thank you,' she replied.

'Do you have plans?' Anthony asked after he had taken a sip of his wine.

'Darius tells me the water taxi should be operational in the morning.'

'Good news indeed. Will you be catching it?'

'I'm not sure.' Zara felt reluctant to update Anthony on her schedule. 'But I expect Owen will return to the mainland at the first opportunity.'

'And Mertice Yo, does she still feature in your plans?'

'I would like to try to visit her once more, if she will speak to me,' Zara said. 'It all depends on my boss.'

'What does this boss of yours do?'

'Research.' Zara kept her answer suitably vague. 'I am his personal assistant.'

'And he sends you round the world?'

'This is the furthest I have been on an assignment, but he knew I had been here before and he thought it would be a good idea if I revisited old haunts.'

'Going back is not always a good idea.'

'It was unfortunate timing.' Zara made a gesture of dismissal and changed the subject. 'If you want to speak to Owen I can pass on a message.'

'Would you apologise to him for me? And,' Anthony continued, 'if you would like to stay on a little longer I could always do with an extra pair of hands.'

'I'm not sure.' Zara stood up, unwilling to commit.

'I promise there will be no repetition of my earlier behaviour.' Anthony also rose to his feet. 'And now I will bid you goodnight. Should you change your mind you know where to contact me.'

* * *

'Where have you been?' Duncan's image appeared on her laptop as Zara sat down on her bed. 'And what happened to your report?'

Duncan was a workaholic and although it was growing late he was still at his desk.

Zara often wondered if he had a private life.

'I've been working on it,' she replied, 'but I haven't been able to contact Mertice Yo. She has a ferocious dog and there's this strange monk-type person, Father Anthony, hanging around.'

'Why do you think he's strange?'

'He keeps popping up all over the place and he verbally abused some poor man who happened to pass by.'

'Could be interesting . . . Have you anything else to report?'

'The water taxi has been out of action.'

'Meaning?'

'Meaning,' Zara kept her voice steady, 'Owen has been unable to get back to the mainland. Thanks for sending him out here, by the way.'

Duncan wasn't into guilt trips but Zara could see the expression of discomfort on his face.

'He needed to track you down urgently.'

Zara leaned back against her pillow. She knew going over old ground wouldn't be any good.

'Well, you've wasted your time,' she said.

'What do you mean?'

'I've lost the paper I was supposed to

sign. Owen and I had a major row. He's gone off somewhere and I don't think I'll be seeing him again as the water taxi should be up and running by tomorrow. Is that a good enough report for you?'

'It's not exactly what I had in mind,' Duncan replied in a dry voice.

'What do you want me to do?' Zara was running out of ideas.

'I'll give you a couple more days to try to fix something up with Mertice. If it doesn't happen you're to come home. Agreed?'

'Agreed.'

Zara was about to finish the call but before she could Duncan spoke again.

'By the way, if you should happen to bump into Owen, tell him Mossy has flown off to Africa to visit her settlement. She's with Sir Robert.'

* * *

Frowning, Zara stood under the shower trying to remember why the name Sir Robert was familiar to her. As she was in bed it came to her. He was Mossy's childhood friend and he had also been the senior judge at the court hearing held in Zara's absence.

As she drifted off to sleep she heard the sound of another car being driven very slowly through the village.

Sinister Appearance

The next morning, still with no sign of Owen, Zara assumed he must have taken the first water taxi of the day back to the mainland. Through the open window she could hear all the usual noises of Xena Island waking up to another busy day.

A weight lifted off her shoulders as the possibility of seeing Owen again was no longer an issue. If he wanted his wretched form signed he was going to have to get a duplicate. Where or when it would be signed was something she could sort out later.

The bar was deserted and there was no sound from the kitchen. Zara suspected Stan wouldn't appreciate being disturbed if he had arrived back and, with no Darius to serve breakfast, she grabbed a quick black coffee from the machine.

Last night's exchange with Duncan had re-energised her. She needed to focus on the reason she had been sent out here in the first place, not worry about ex-husbands and lost paperwork. Gulping down her gritty coffee she had a rethink and decided to take Anthony up on his offer.

The morning sun was warm on her back as she strode up the hill, her pace slackening off when the incline grew steeper.

Anthony was working in his herb garden in front of his whitewashed house and hearing Zara approach he stood up, a smile of welcome on his face.

'You have come to join me?'

'I can spare an hour if you need help.'

Zara decided having Anthony as an ally would be a better strategy than antagonising him. He had apologised for his outburst and she could appreciate from her own personal experience how mood swings could change in an instant so she decided to treat the matter as history.

'Weeds.' Anthony sighed. 'The curse of a herbalist's life.' He passed her a long-handled hoe. 'Would you like to start at the far end? We can meet in the middle.'

Zara worked diligently, welcoming the combined tang of lemon and mint as she disturbed the oregano and thyme. Hoeing helped to clear her head and prodding around in the dusty earth was excellent therapy for relieving her pent-up feelings over Owen. The scraping sound of Anthony's hoe grew closer as he moved along the line.

'Anthony,' Zara said when he was near enough for her to speak to him without shouting. He paused for breath leaning on his hoe and wiped his face with a spotless white handkerchief.

'More questions?' There was the trace of a smile in his voice and none of the previous day's petulance.

'Who do you think drives through the village late at night?'

He looked startled by her question.

'Why do you ask?'

'I'm sure a car passed your house the night we spent with you and last night I heard it again.'

'You weren't dreaming?'

'Absolutely not.'
'How can you be sure it's the same car?' Anthony's question stumped Zara. To an outsider her suspicions would sound foolish.
'I hadn't fallen asleep so I wasn't dreaming.'
'You have not answered my question.'
'I suppose I don't know if it was the same car,' Zara was forced to admit.
'I can't help you, I'm afraid,' Anthony sounded sympathetic. 'I have a bicycle. One or two of the younger set have the use of cars but most people come here for the water sports. There are very few motorised vehicles on the island.'
'Does Mertice own a car?'
'There is an old outhouse in the grounds.' He appeared to choose his words carefully. 'But I haven't been inside it.'
Zara frowned. When it came to talking about Mertice, Anthony seemed reluctant to answer direct questions.
'So you don't know?'
Anthony shrugged.

'When did you last see Mertice?' Zara persisted with her line of questioning.

A beeping sound came to Anthony's rescue. He delved into the pockets of his voluminous robe.

'You see,' he produced a smartphone, 'we are not entirely at odds with modern life.' Extracting a pair of glasses from his other pocket he peered at the screen and made a tutting noise. 'I am sorry, my dear Zara, an appointment I cannot ignore.'

'You're leaving?'

'I shouldn't be long. Would you like to finish up here? You will find fresh apple tea in the kitchen if you require refreshment. Make yourself at home. I will be back as soon as I can.'

Retrieving his battered bicycle from against a low stone wall he hitched up his robe, gave a quick ring of goodbye on his bell before pedalling off furiously in the direction of the village. Zara listened to the swish of his tyres on the bumpy ground as he disappeared into the distance.

Feeling she had been outmanoeuvred,

she collected Anthony's fallen hoe. There was no doubt the unexpected interruption had come at a very convenient time for him. She couldn't help wondering if by some sleight of hand Anthony had arranged to set off an alarm on his phone and invented a fake appointment to get away from her line of questioning.

Shaking her head in dismissal she finished off the last of her weeding. Half an hour later, thirsty and hot, she made her way up to the house.

The white walls dazzled in the sunlight, blinding her, but the kitchen was cool and clean and Zara welcomed the change in atmosphere and temperature. Rinsing dirt off her hands in the sink she looked around for a towel.

Her eyes alighted on a fringed shawl draped over the back of a chair. She inhaled a delicate jasmine fragrance as she picked it up. It reminded her of summer fields and lazy days when it was too hot to do anything.

She ran her fingers over the designer logo embroidered in a corner of the shawl. It was one she could not identify. Her fingers tightened around the shawl. At last she had stumbled on something of significance.

She sat down at the table and sipped fresh apple tea while she tried to rearrange her thoughts into a semblance of order.

At some time Anthony must have entertained a female visitor. That would explain why he didn't want to answer personal questions and why he was brusque with strangers.

Zara hadn't given much thought to the exact nature of his beliefs or whether his wearing of a monk's habit was a self-imposed discipline, but from her limited knowledge of sects she believed many did not allow relationships with the opposite sex.

To all appearances Anthony lived alone but Zara's convictions grew more certain by the minute. The voice she had heard talking to Anthony the night she and Owen had stayed over was female.

Zara allowed the delicate material of

the shawl to slip through her fingers. It was a chic accessory worn by a woman with a sense of style. Who on the island would own such an item of clothing?

Most of the women spent their days working in the markets, gutting fish or serving drinks and meals at the numerous tavernas dotted along the coast. They would have no use for a shawl of this nature but one name sprang to Zara's mind — Mertice Yo.

A shadow fell across the table. Zara spun round. Standing in the doorway was Ned Tripp.

'What are you doing?' He snatched the shawl out of Zara's hands.

'Nothing.' She recoiled.

'This belongs to Mertice.'

'How do you know?'

'I've seen her wearing it.'

'Well, I didn't know it belonged to her.' Zara kept her voice neutral but it proved impossible to control the rapid beating of her pulse.

Ned paced up and down the kitchen seemingly unable to stand still.

'Where's Anthony?' His pale eyes flickered around the kitchen.

'He had an appointment.'

'He's with her again, isn't he?'

'Who?'

'He was with her yesterday. I caught them together but her horrid dog chased me away.

'They can't keep me out. I'll be back.' He blinked rapidly and pushed his glasses back up the bridge of his nose.

'Yes, well, like I said, Anthony isn't here and I have to be going.'

'I have to see her.'

He clutched the back of a wooden chair the knuckles of his bony hands protruding.

Zara couldn't help noticing that like many wiry people he possessed surprising physical strength.

'If you'll excuse me,' she prompted, but Ned didn't budge and there was no way Zara could get past him. He was now standing with his back to the door.

'Did you know she was a prima ballerina?'

'You know Mertice, do you?' Zara was thinking on her feet. If she handled Ned right it was possible he could be an ally.

'She won't see me.' Ned dashed Zara's hopes. 'She won't see anyone except Father Anthony.'

'Is she close to Father Anthony?'

'They visit each other at night. Sometimes she drives down from her villa or Father Anthony cycles up to see her. I've seen them coming and going.'

A prickle of apprehension inched up Zara's spine. The idea of Ned spying on Anthony and Mertice was unsettling.

'Did you know Iannis Theodorous?' Zara tried a diversionary tactic.

'I have to see Mertice,' Ned repeated, an obstinate look on his face.

'Is it something to do with Iannis?'

'You don't understand.' Ned cast Zara a disparaging look and for the first time since they had met Zara was in total agreement with him.

'Why don't you enlighten me?' she coaxed adding, 'Mertice inherited Iannis's property portfolio when he died, didn't she?'

'She is so beautiful.' Ned seemed to have difficulty concentrating. 'I can understand why Iannis fell in love with her.'

'Were you a victim of the fraud?' Forgetting her apprehension, Zara leaned in towards Ned.

'We are all victims one way or another.'

Zara stifled her impatience. When it came to discussing Mertice, everyone clammed up.

'Why do you want to see Mertice?' she asked.

'Out of my way.'

Ned pushed past the man standing behind him in the doorway.

'Owen?' Zara sagged in relief.

'Are you OK?' He was by her side in an instant.

'I'm fine. Thanks for the rescue.'

'That character is seriously disturbed. He didn't harm you?'

'He just talked a load of nonsense.' Zara drew away from him. 'What are you doing here?'

'I came looking for you.'

'If this is about our divorce . . .' Zara took a deep breath.

'No, it isn't. Here, sit down.' Owen pushed Zara into a chair. 'Now what is going on?'

'You tell me,' Zara retaliated. 'Where were you last night?'

'I went over to Xylon; it's the neighbouring island to Xena.'

'Why?'

'I'll tell you in a minute. When I got back I caught up with Darius. He told me Anthony dropped by the taverna last night and he thought you were probably up here. Where is Anthony, by the way?'

'We were weeding the herbs when he got an urgent call. I don't know where he went.'

'No matter.'

'He was full of apologies for the incident with Ned.'

Owen brushed aside her explanation. 'I want you to come to Xylon with me.'

'What for?'

'I've learned some interesting things

about Iannis Theodorous which I think you should hear first hand. The water taxi can get us there in half an hour.'

'What about Anthony?'

'You can leave him a note. Come on, we haven't much time.'

Keeping up Appearances

Xylon was the smaller twin to Xena. As the caïque ploughed through the water towards their destination Zara listened to the young pilot delivering a potted history of the island.

'I am born here,' he announced with pride, 'and it is the best place in the world to live.'

'You don't miss the night clubs and bright lights of the other islands?' Owen enquired with a tolerant smile.

'What would I do with them? My days are spent in the open air and I have no need of loud music or fights.'

'Surely not fights,' Zara protested.

'But yes,' Eduardo's smile slackened off. 'It does happen. There is occasionally trouble on Xena, so I stay on Xylon. I am happy. I have a girlfriend, a family and a job. What more could I want?'

'What more indeed,' Owen agreed.

Zara leaned back against the side of the boat. On their walk down to the landing stage Owen had told her Xylon wasn't popular with tourists, mainly because it didn't promote itself as a holiday island. It was no more than a dot on the map and nestled in the shadow of its jetset neighbours.

'If you look hard,' Owen now pointed in the distance, 'you can make out the coastline of Xylon.'

'Is it so very different from Xena?' Zara asked.

'It's unique,' Owen replied. 'The islanders are proud of their heritage and it has a style of its own. Its beaches are deserted even in the height of the holiday season and everyday life evolved around the traditional trades of boat building, fishing and the cultivation of olives.'

'Surely they want visitors.' Zara frowned.

'There's a commune tucked away in a quiet corner of the harbour. It's where specialist artists go to learn about the history of vase painting.'

'Vase painting has a history?'

'Don't let Eduardo see you looking

so surprised. It's the only big business the island can lay claim to. There are different styles and shapes and the images used to decorate the ancient works of art have a special symbolism.

'Few people are aware of the island's existence and even fewer take the time to visit. Tourists aren't unwelcome but apart from water sports and archaeological tours there's little to attract the crowds.'

Zara shaded her eyes against the fierce sun as they approached the harbour. The terracotta tiles of the harbourside dwellings reflected dull gold in the heat of the early afternoon, the earthy base colour a sharp contrast to the blue water slapping the side of their boat. Exotic fish darted around their bows escorting them to the mooring point.

'Your first sight of Xylon is a moment to be savoured.' Owen's voice interrupted Zara's enjoyment of the slow-moving solitude that typified Xylon life.

'Your friend lives here?' she asked in an envious voice.

'Conrad Desoutter. He's American, his wife Demi is Greek. When his first marriage broke up he decided to opt out of the rat race. He was something of a high flyer in the old days. I suppose you could say he suffered burn out. Anyway, he met Demi on a transatlantic flight — she used to be air crew — they got together and,' Owen indicated the harbour, 'this is the result.'

'What does he do now?'

'Demi is a brilliant cook and runs a private catering company. It's not big business but she enjoys it. Conrad helps her. He also pilots the occasional water taxi around the other islands just to keep his hand in.'

'It sounds idyllic,' Zara said.

'Please?' Eduardo indicated to Owen. 'It is safe now to disembark.'

'There he is,' Owen waved enthusiastically to where a lean-limbed man wearing battered shorts, white shirt and straw hat stood waiting for them. 'Come on.'

Owen grabbed Zara's hand and before

she could protest pulled her along the harbour. The two men slapped palms in greeting before Conrad turned his attention to Zara.

'Hi, Conrad Desoutter.' He held out his hand. 'Zara, isn't it? Pleased to meet you.' His grip was firm and Zara immediately warmed towards him. 'Let's get the show on the road,' he said releasing his hold. 'Meet Persephone.'

'I thought your wife was called Demi,' Zara said, looking round.

Conrad's smile stretched across his face in a wide grin.

'This is Persephone,' he indicated a battered pick-up truck. 'Don't let appearances fool you.' Conrad caught the doubtful look Zara cast towards their intended transport.

'My gal here is great for deliveries and chores and she hasn't let me down, not once.' He held open the cab door. 'Hop in. 'Fraid it's a bit of a squash up front but it's not far. Nowhere is far from anywhere on Xylon. Great place, don't you think? I fell in love with the island the first time I saw it. Demi, you'll love her as much as I do, she comes from the island and she doesn't ever want to leave.'

Conrad kept up a constant stream of patter as he crunched gears and swung the pick-up truck around hairpin bends. On more than one occasion Zara closed her eyes in fear for her life.

The only oncoming traffic they met was a cart loaded with melons, the driver giving a cheerful wave as they passed him with less than a hair's breadth between them and a young lad leading a pannier-laden donkey towards a small market selling fresh fruit and fish.

It was as they drew up in front of a streamlined dazzling whitewashed building that Zara realised she had been clutching Owen's hand.

'You can let go now,' he murmured in her ear, 'we've arrived.'

Flushing with embarrassment, Zara fought down the urge to admit Conrad's driving was not an experience she cared to repeat.

A petite dark-haired woman was

waiting for them on the front step of the house.

'You've arrived.' Her smile was as welcoming as Conrad's. She beamed at Zara as she climbed out of the cab and kissed her on both cheeks. 'What wonderful hair, burnished gold. I am so envious. No wonder Owen fell in love with you. I am almost in love with you myself.' She laughed, linking arms with Conrad. 'Don't you think Zara is beautiful, darling?'

'Not as beautiful as you,' he replied gallantly.

Zara cast Owen a questioning look wondering what he had told his friend about their marital status.

'And you are on a second honeymoon? What a wonderful idea,' Demi enthused. 'Perhaps Conrad and I will have one after we have been married for ten years.'

Owen had the grace to look shamefaced and gave an imperceptible shrug as Zara cast him a look of disbelief.

'Come in.' Demi ushered them towards the house. 'It's too hot to stand outside talking. I have made fresh mint tea and if you can smell herbs it will be my traditional stew. I like the flavour of the dill to be absorbed so I cook it slowly to seal in the juices. I hope you are hungry.'

Demi talked as much as Conrad and luckily did not appear to require any answer to her questions.

'You would like to freshen up?' She indicated a bathroom. 'We'll be out on the terrace when you are ready.'

'What was all that about a second honeymoon?' Zara hissed at Owen as she rinsed her hands and face with cold water.

Owen continued to look shamefaced. 'Sorry. I didn't mean to land you in it but you've seen Conrad and Demi, it's difficult to get a word in edgewise. They know you're my wife and as technically we are still married I kept up the pretence. Do you think you could go with the flow for the evening?'

'You're even beginning to sound like Conrad.' Zara attempted to run a comb through her hair but the wind coming off the water had reduced it to an unruly mass.

'It's catching, isn't it?' Owen grinned back at her. He looked relaxed and younger and Zara caught a trace of the man she fell in love with. 'Ready?'

'As I'll ever be but don't expect me to go all lovey-dovey. I'm not carrying the pretence that far.'

'I'm pleased to hear it,' Owen agreed. 'Come on, we'd better get back outside, otherwise Demi will think we're kissing or something.'

'There's no need to keep hold of my hand,' Zara insisted.

'Force of habit.' Owen released his hold and held open the bathroom door, allowing her to go through first.

'I was about to send out a search party,' Demi greeted them with an arch smile. 'Are you both refreshed enough to drink some mint tea?' She poured out two glasses.

'Now if the three of you are going to talk business there are one or two things in the kitchen I have to attend to. The commune is holding a party tomorrow night and they want traditional Greek dishes. Zara, if the men get too technical come and join me.'

'OK, honey.' Conrad's eyes followed Demi as she left the terrace. 'Don't worry about joining her, Zara, in the kitchen Demi is a demon, she works better alone. I've learned from personal experience life is a lot calmer if I leave her to it.' Conrad narrowed his eyes.

'Right, down to the reason for the visit. Owen tells me you're interested in learning about Iannis Theodorous.'

'The thing is,' Owen interrupted, 'we can't get to see Mertice Yo.'

'I can't get to see her,' Zara corrected him.

'Why do you need to?'

'My boss is interested in a possible documentary on the island and I thought a good place to start would be with Mertice.'

Conrad glanced questioningly at Owen as if wondering why Zara would want to work on her second honeymoon. When no explanation was forthcoming he continued.

'Well, I don't know much about Mertice apart from what I've read in the press so we won't go there.'

'And Iannis?' Zara prompted.

'Now there's a man I do know something about. Iannis Theodorous was a financier. He ran a fancy investment firm. It wasn't all it was cut out to be and he was about to be arrested for fraud when he died unexpectedly of a heart attack.'

'On Xena,' Owen put in.

'Right,' Conrad agreed. 'Apparently Iannis fled to the island to get away from the financial authorities. I'm not sure where he was previously based. I guess his career was global and he travelled a lot. His lifestyle probably contributed to his health issues.'

'When did he die?' Zara asked.

'About five years ago, I think. You didn't know any of this?'

Zara shook her head. Owen had insisted they take a break from all social media during their honeymoon and once they were home they had other things on their minds.

'Mertice inherited Iannis's substantial property portfolio,' Conrad continued, 'and for a while she was the subject of official enquiries. Nothing could ever be proven against her. I believe the file on Iannis is still open but investigations have been scaled down. So there you have it.'

'Mertice Yo wasn't involved in Iannis's business affairs?'

'Seems not. I understand she was a dancer?' Conrad queried.

'A prima ballerina,' Zara corrected him.

'Sure, well, like I said, she got the property but not the money.'

'And you wouldn't have any idea why Mertice and Father Anthony meet up after dark?'

'He's the guy Owen was telling me about, the one who grows herbs and stuff?'

'Yes.'

'I've no idea what he gets up to after dark.'

'Do you know anything about him at all?' Zara asked.

'I have never met him but Demi is another of Stan's cousins and whenever the family visit they bring us some of his produce. Sorry I can't be of any more help.' Conrad glanced over Zara's shoulder.

'If you're finished, Zara, I can see Demi making gestures at us. I think dinner is ready. I don't know about you but I'm hungry enough to eat a bear so we'd best not keep her waiting.'

Shocking Discovery

Conrad and Demi were generous hosts, regaling Owen and Zara with stories of life on the island and how they had adapted to the lifestyle change.

'I used to fly around the world,' Demi said while trying unsuccessfully to persuade Zara to indulge in a third helping of stew, 'and Conrad lived in New York.'

He shuddered.

'Looking back I wonder how we survived the frantic pace of life.'

'So you don't miss it?' Owen enquired.

Conrad gestured towards the view outside the window. Their dining area overlooked an olive farm and in the distance Zara could see a hillside studded with brightly coloured wild flowers.

'Would you?' Conrad asked. 'There isn't a hi-tech concrete block in sight.'

'We have everything we want,' Demi looked lovingly at Conrad.

'We work hard,' Conrad explained, 'but somehow it doesn't seem like work.

Am I making sense?'

Demi looked questioningly at Zara.

'Conrad tells me you still work?'

'Yes,' Zara's discomfort increased. She hoped Demi wouldn't ask too many personal questions. It was difficult keeping up the pretence of her and Owen being a happily married couple.

'You must miss Owen when he is away,' she smiled across the table.

Owen came to her rescue.

'Zara enjoys her job. She would be lost without it.'

Zara cast him a grateful look.

'You have never thought of giving it up?' Demi persisted.

'Hey,' Conrad intervened, 'give the girl a rest.'

'I was thinking if Zara likes the sunshine she could join us here. I could always use an extra pair of hands and it doesn't matter where you are based, does it, Owen? You could relocate.'

'Who knows what the future holds?' was Owen's enigmatic reply.

'Sure thing,' Conrad agreed. 'My life

turned round in the space of a week.'

Zara gulped. Her life had been full of life-changing moments recently, all including Owen.

Demi lit a mood candle and placed it on the table as the light faded from the day. The amber flame cast a gentle glow on the evening.

'I hope you like your room,' she said. 'It's recently been refurbished.'

'Room?' Zara jerked herself back to the present.

'We've put you in the guest bedroom.'

'We're not staying overnight.' The drumming noise in Zara's ears threatened to deafen her.

'You have no choice,' Conrad drawled. 'The taxis don't operate after nightfall.'

'But I haven't brought anything with me and neither has Owen.'

Zara looked to him for help but Owen looked equally lost for words.

'No problem. I can provide all you need,' Demi replied. 'Now why don't the two of you stay and finish the wine while I sort out some essentials for you?

Conrad,' she nudged him with her elbow, 'Owen needs a toothbrush.'

'Sure he does.' Conrad rolled his eyes and stood up. 'OK, honey, I can take a hint. See you guys in the morning.'

'What do we do now?' Zara hissed at Owen when they were alone.

'As Demi suggests, we finish the wine.'

'We can't spend the night together.'

'We'll have to keep up the deception for a few more hours.'

'Why didn't you tell Conrad the truth?'
'You must have noticed he's a difficult guy to interrupt. The moment didn't arise.

His first marriage didn't end well and now he's so happy I didn't want to burst his bubble.'

'This is an impossible situation.'

A smile tugged at the corner of Owen's mouth.

'At the risk of imitating Conrad why don't you chill and enjoy the moment?'

Zara gulped down a large mouthful of wine in an attempt to steady her nerves.

The shadows were lengthening and the

amber flame from Demi's mood candle flickered steadily against the encroaching night.

Zara stared into its depths. She still owed Owen a decent apology and she needed to get it off her chest.

'I didn't mean what I said about you having stability issues,' she began in a small voice, unable to look Owen in the eye.

'I've had worse said to me,' Owen's gravelly voice sent a tingle down Zara's spine. 'Besides, I started the stability issues thing so maybe I should be the one apologising to you.'

She curbed the urge to reach out and touch his hand. He had never been one to hold a grudge and she remembered how impossible it had been to have a disagreement with him. Taking a deep breath she ploughed on.

'And I don't know what happened to the paper you asked me to sign.'

'What's a lost piece of paper between friends?'

'Is that what we are — friends?'

'I hope we'll always be something more than friends.'

'I don't see how we can be.'

'Why not?'

'Mossy would have to be a pretty special person to want me around.'

'She is special. Her charity work is something else.'

'I forgot to tell you!' Zara put a horrified hand to her mouth. 'Duncan asked me to pass on a message. Mossy and Sir Robert have flown out together to Africa.'

Owen nodded.

'Right.'

'Are you going to join her?'

'We'll see.'

'I'm sorry if I've held up your return.'

'It was my decision to fly out here, so don't beat yourself up about it.'

'Are you quite sure Sir Robert didn't make a mistake about the status of our divorce?'

'Cast iron, I'm afraid, so that's something else I am going to have to take the blame for.'

Zara turned her attention back to the candle. The wick was smouldering as it burned down.

'The demands on Mossy's time are constant — that's why I wanted to get everything fixed up before she took off on her travels again but no matter.'

'If you were expecting to meet up some time soon I don't think it's going to happen,' Zara said. 'Duncan intimated she could be away for a while.'

'We're rarely in the same place at the same time.' Owen inspected the contents of his wine glass. 'Our schedules are frequently disrupted. I can handle it.'

He flashed Zara a smile but it didn't quite reach his eyes.

'What will you do after you're married?'

'Do?'

'Where do you intend to live?'

'It's a tricky one. With Mossy's commitments it won't be easy, so we shall have to see. Maybe I'll do spontaneous, as Conrad suggests. Give up my career and retire to Cornwall. Flying is a young man's game.'

'Does the rising sun still paint the harbour wall?' A faraway look came into Zara's eyes.

'It hasn't changed its routine. Neither have I. I still enjoy breakfast on the balcony even when it's blowing a gale.'

'Do you remember the day we nearly lost our coffee pot, and the bad-tempered seagull who mugged you?' A dimple dented Zara's cheek. 'You were mad as a badger when it swooped and pinched a slice of toast out of your hand.'

Owen grinned.

'Unlike you, I didn't see the funny side at the time but we both laughed about it afterwards. We laughed a lot in those days.'He was silent for a moment. 'We did get one or two things right during our marriage, didn't we?'

'We did.' Zara's eyes softened at the memory. She wished Own wouldn't look at her so intently.

The flame from the candle gave a final flicker.

'If you've finished your wine,' he said

in a brisk voice, 'we'd best check out this guest room of Demi's.'

With her heart thumping painfully in her chest Zara made her way up the stone steps to the guest bedroom. It was on the third floor and to her relief it was a twin bedded room. Demi had laid out a cotton nightdress and overnight toiletries.

'I might sleep on the balcony,' Owen slid open the glass door. 'There's a sun lounger out here.'Have you got everything you need?'

'Thank you, yes.'

'I'll see you in the morning. Sleep well.'

Despite expectations, Zara had a dreamless sleep, not waking up until Owen tapped on the window.

'Can I come in?' he enquired. 'Demi's on her way up with some coffee so I'll dive in the shower.'

Before Zara could say anything Owen scooted across the floor and into the bathroom.

'I know you need to get back as soon

as possible,' Demi deposited the breakfast tray on a small table, 'so when you are ready Conrad will run you down to the harbour for the water taxi.' She cocked an ear.

'Owen seems happy. It must be the fresh air,' she said with a knowing smile.

The sound of him singing badly and off key reminded Zara of how he used to like to exercise his vocal cords in the bath. She vividly remembered banging on the bathroom door and telling him to stop disturbing the neighbours.

She poured out a cup of hot strong coffee. The sooner Owen headed back to the mainland the better. Being this close to him was reviving far too many memories of the good times.

Those days were gone. Owen was now engaged to Mossy and once he and Zara finalised their divorce he could marry his beautiful model fiancée with a clear conscience.

'Come again soon,' Conrad insisted after another white-knuckle ride in Persephone.

The harbour was a haven of early morning activity and Zara and Owen had to pick their way over fishermen mending nets and grading their catch ready for the market.

'Thank goodness that's over,' Owen stood beside Zara on the deck of their caïque waving to Conrad as it eased out of the harbour. 'I don't think I could have kept up the act of enjoying a second honeymoon much longer.'

'I hope they didn't suspect anything,' Zara said.

'Demi's got a keen eye and I reckon she would have sussed us out had we stayed any longer.' He looked up at the sky. 'I'm going to try to get a signal and see if I can contact Mossy. You OK?'

'Fine.' Zara gripped the rail as she kept her gaze on Xylon's disappearing coastline.

Half an hour later and back on Xena, Zara spotted an agitated Stan pacing up and down outside the taverna.

'What's wrong?' Zara asked as he hurried towards them.

'Father Anthony,' he began. 'He hasn't done his morning round. I can't raise him on his mobile. It is unlike him not to contact me if he's going to be delayed.'

'Do you want us to go and check on him?' Owen volunteered.

'I am expecting several deliveries,' Stan explained. 'I cannot leave the taverna unattended.'

'I'll go,' Zara volunteered.

'We'll go together,' Owen insisted.

'You need to get back to the mainland.'

'With Mossy away there's no rush.'

'I hope Ned Tripp hasn't come back and made trouble.' Zara was having difficulty keeping up with Owen's long strides. 'You know he's been spying on Anthony and Mertice?'

'No, I didn't. Why didn't you tell me earlier?'

'I was somewhat preoccupied with your friends Conrad and Demi. Besides, do you need to know?'

'Perhaps something has been going on between Anthony and Mertice.'

'That's what I've been trying to tell

you. Anthony cycles everywhere but the other night I definitely heard a vehicle outside Stan's taverna. It was very late.'

'I fail to see the connection to Anthony.'

'It sounded like the car I heard outside his house the night we slept over.'

Owen looked unconvinced.

'Connection or not Anthony knows more than he's telling us.'

'How do you know?'

'Mertice left her shawl in his kitchen. Ned recognised it when he turned up. He also went on about her being so beautiful and a lot of other stuff I didn't take on board. He might have opened up with something useful if he hadn't taken off when he did.'

They reached Anthony's house and Owen banged on the door.

'Can you hear anything?' he demanded.

'No.'

'Stand back,' Owen ordered.

'You can't break in,' Zara protested.

The door splintered as Owen put his shoulder to it.

'Anthony,' Zara shrieked racing over

to where he was lying on the floor. 'Can you hear me?' She placed two fingers on Anthony's wrist then turned an agonised face to Owen. 'I can't find a pulse.'

Revelations

Owen crashed around the kitchen, scattering neatly stacked papers in a frantic search for a telephone.

'There must be a landline somewhere. I can't get a signal on my mobile.'

'Anthony's not breathing.' Zara was doing her best to quell her rising panic.

Owen strode to the door.

'I'll borrow Anthony's bicycle.'

'Where are you going?'

'Mertice must have a telephone. Will you be OK on your own?'

'Look out for the dog.' Zara's voice was drowned by the sound of Owen dragging Anthony's bicycle out from the tool shed. 'Zara?' A faint cry came from the floor.

'Anthony!' She squeezed his hand. 'Can you tell me what happened?' she asked gently. 'Did you have a fall?'

'No . . . ' His eyelids fluttered. He tried to speak but it was too much of an effort to talk and he lapsed back into unconsciousness.

'Stay with me,' Zara urged, clutching his hand. 'Owen has gone for help. He won't be long.'

In spite of the heat of the day Anthony's hand was icy. As Zara grabbed a rug and draped it over his prostrate form, a sheet of paper Owen had disturbed drifted to the ground. Zara anchored it down with her backpack.

Anthony's breathing was ragged but his pulse was now steady.

'Help is on its way.'

His forehead felt clammy as Zara stroked his face hoping he could hear her.

'What's going on?'

Zara stifled a shriek of surprise at the sound of a voice behind her. Framed in the doorway Ned Tripp was inspecting the damage. He ran a finger over the splintered wood.

'Has there been a break in?' There was a note of suspicion in his voice.

'You tell me,' Zara snapped back.

'What's happened to Father Anthony?' Behind his horn-rimmed glasses Ned's eyes were full of concern as he looked to where Father Anthony lay on the floor.

'We found him like this.'

Ned took a tentative step forward.

'He's had an attack. Where are his tablets?'

'What tablets?'

'He's on medication for an irregular heartbeat.'

'How do you know?'

'The doctor told me.'

'I don't believe you. He'd be forbidden from giving out a patient's medical details.'

A tinge of pink stained Ned's pale cheeks.

'I bumped into him on his rounds. He's the only person on the island who would talk to me. The wind caught one of his prescriptions. I raced after it and picked it up. I saw the name on the top and I recognised what the pills were for. Now do you believe me?'

Realising this was not the time to go into the morals of the situation Zara cast her eyes around the kitchen. Apart from the papers disturbed by Owen everything was where it should be. There wasn't so much as a plate out of place.

'Do you have any idea where Anthony keeps his medication?'

'That belongs to Drosselmeyer.' Ned eyed up the rug Zara had used to make Anthony more comfortable. 'He likes to stretch out on it in the sun.'

'Focus.' Zara fought down the urge to shake Ned by his skinny shoulders. 'Anthony's doctor?'

'What about him?'

'You said you knew him.'

'I knew the locum. He was standing in for the regular doctor but he's gone back to the mainland. I've no idea who Anthony goes to now.'

Zara wanted to scream with frustration. This was getting her nowhere.

Zara felt movement under the rug as Anthony stirred.

'Anthony,' Zara bent over him, 'where are your tablets?'

There was no response.

'Ned, can you go and get help?' She

spoke slowly and clearly suspecting he wouldn't respond to physical intimidation.

'I had such trouble finding Mertice and now she won't talk to me.' He sounded as though he had drifted off into a world of his own.

'No-one on the island talks to me any more. It took me ages to pluck up the courage to speak to Father Anthony and when I did he shouted at me. I don't know what to do.'

'Do you have some form of transport I could borrow?' Zara raised her voice in an attempt to get through to him.

'No.'

'Where are you staying?'

'I camp out at night.'

'How do you get round the island?'

'I walk,' he explained. 'I go out early in the morning before most people are up. Most days I see Anthony cycling back here or Mertice driving home. Is that what you want to know?'

'Right now I need physical help.'

'And that's not all I see.' Ned's eyes

were bright with excitement.

'Listen to me, Ned,' Zara implored, 'this is an emergency.'

'You're like everyone else. You won't listen to me.'

'Ned, wait.'

Turning on his heel he strode out of the kitchen. Zara mentally tried to calculate how long it would take Owen to cycle up to Mertice's house. She had lost track of time but she couldn't wait much longer. If Owen couldn't get through to Mertice Zara would have to go for help.

Staggering to her feet she poured out a glass of water and kneeling down tried to get Anthony to take a few sips before standing up again and yanking open the overhead units without success.

'Anthony.' She knelt over him, 'I'm going for help. I won't be long. I'll check the bathroom first and if I can't find your tablets there I'll be off.'

Zara had gone no further than halfway down the corridor before she heard a loud crash from the kitchen followed by the ferocious barking of a dog.

'Be quiet,' Owen's voice thundered.

With her heart beating a tattoo, Zara raced back to the kitchen.

A petite woman was crouched over Anthony, cradling his head in her hands.

'Thank heavens you're back.' Zara sagged against the wall. Her legs were shaking.

'What have you been doing to him?' The woman crouching beside Anthony glared at her.

'Nothing, we found him like this.'

'He's soaking wet.'

'I tried to get him to drink some water.'

'Why were you creeping around the house?'

'I was looking for tablets. Ned Tripp told me Anthony was on medication.'

'The one with glasses and skinny legs — he is mad!' The woman made a dismissive gesture. 'I will deal with this. Please leave — now,' she insisted.

'You haven't told me who you are.' Zara stood her ground, fully aware of the woman's identity but wanting to hear it confirmed.

The woman's eyes flared.

'I am Mertice Yo,' she announced with a regal toss of her head. Zara felt as though she had been punched in the stomach as she added, 'and Father Anthony is my husband.'

Signed and Sealed

Zara stumbled, coming into contact with Owen's broad chest.

'Steady,' he cautioned solid as a rock in front of her while Zara disentangled her body from his. 'What on earth made you wear those ridiculous sandals? One of your buckle's is loose.' He looked down at her footwear in disgust. 'You'd be much better off with mountain boots.'

Zara opened her mouth to protest but she didn't have the energy to argue and the sensible half of her brain was telling her Owen was right.

'Mertice and Anthony, did I hear right? They're married?'

'Looks like it,' Owen acknowledged with a wry smile.

'I think Mertice regretted telling us. Did you notice how she couldn't get shot of us quick enough?'

'There was no reason for us to stay. We'd done our bit.'

Owen was scanning the horizon as he

spoke.

'What are you looking for?'

The reflection of the turquoise sea against the sun was blinding. Surfers were out in full force showing off their skills as they crested the waves dodging past the fishing boats ploughing back into the harbour.

'The water taxi.'

'Why?'

Owen fixed his dark eyes on Zara's.

'Mertice doesn't want us here and she's right. I think we both need to get off the island, the sooner the better.'

The wailing siren of an ambulance echoing in the distance sent an inexplicable shiver down Zara's spine.

'I'll go when I'm ready,' Zara insisted and continued before Owen could remonstrate. 'How did you manage to get past Mertice's security?'

Owen's shamefaced smile curved the corners of his mouth.

'You don't want to know.'

'I do.'

'It's not something I'm proud of. I

threw stones at Drosselmeyer.'

'You didn't!' Zara was appalled.

'Mertice was down the drive quicker than you can say prima ballerina and accusing me of all sorts of things in a language I didn't understand. She was off like a scalded cat when I finally got a word in and told her about Anthony.'

'I'm thinking now we have officially been introduced to each other I am going to push for an interview,' Zara announced. 'I mean, if it hadn't been for us, Anthony could have been lying there for days.'

Zara bumped into Owen again as he came to a sudden halt.

'You'll do no such thing,' he ordered, 'Haven't you been listening to a word I've said?'

Zara stared at him in outrage.

'You can't stop me. Besides, why should you care about me?'

'You're not going to like this.' He softened his voice. 'I'm worried for your safety.'

Zara made a noise of disbelief at the

back of her throat.

'You're right, I don't like it and for your information I make my own rules. What you like or don't like doesn't come into it.'

They were both breathing heavily as they stared at each other.

'What's bugging you, Owen?' Zara relented.

'I can't put my finger on it,' he admitted, 'but something isn't right.'

'When I tried to tell you the same thing you took no notice. What's changed your mind?'

'I'm serious, Zara.'

'So am I and there's no need to worry about me. I can look after myself.'

'I can't help feeling responsible for all that's happened.'

'The only thing you are responsible for is getting married to Mossy. So you do need to leave the island — immediately.'

'You have to come with me.'

'Subject closed,' Zara insisted, pushing at the door of Stan's taverna.

'There you are!' Stan bounded out eyes alight with excitement. 'I've been looking out for you.'

'Sorry we couldn't deliver updates,' Owen apologised, 'we couldn't get a signal. Father Anthony's been taken to hospital so I don't know when you'll get your next delivery of fresh herbs.'

'No matter.' Stan made a dismissive gesture with his hands.

'What do you mean no matter?' Zara's voice rose in disbelief. 'Father Anthony has been hospitalised.'

'Yes, of course. You are right. It was his heart?'

'You knew about his condition?'

'Sometimes he forgets to take his tablets. They have to stabilise him at the hospital. It is not the first time this has happened.'

'It would have helped if you'd told us all this before.'

'I apologise but now I have more news for you.'

'I need to freshen up.' Zara felt disinclined to listen to anything more Stan had to say.

'There's been an incident down in the harbour,' Stan announced.

'What sort of incident?' Owen prompted.

'You know that strange person — the foreigner who wears big glasses?'

'Ned Tripp?' Zara shook off her apathy, 'What about him?'

'His jacket has been fished out of the harbour.'

'What?'

'How do you know it's his?' Owen demanded.

'Someone identified it. They are also saying he jumped in.'

'He can't have,' Zara gulped, 'I saw him this morning.'

'Was he wearing his jacket?' Owen demanded.

'I don't remember. I was crouched on the floor tending to Anthony.'

'He was perhaps worried about something?' Stan asked.

'He was agitated but he always is. I think he was scared he would be accused of attacking Father Anthony.'

'Reason enough to jump off the harbour wall,' Stan proclaimed.

'Did anybody see him lurking about the waterfront or hear a splash?' Owen asked.

'Midday everyone rests,' Stan explained. 'The fishermen say he was not there when they went for their lunch.'

'Can you remember anything else Ned said?' Owen turned to Zara.

'He rambled on about Mertice and Anthony's medical condition.'

'Is that all?'

'I wasn't paying proper attention. Next thing I knew he accused me of not listening to him and he was gone. I've no idea where he went.'

'He could be anywhere on the island.' Owen squinted into the sunshine, a hopeless look on his face.

'You want to join the search party?' Stan invited.

'Maybe later.'

'If you need me you know where I am.' Stan set off at a jog down the hill towards the harbour.

'That settles it,' Owen hustled Zara into the cool of the bar, 'you're catching the next water taxi out of here.'

'I've told you I decide when I want to leave,' Zara insisted.

'Ned Tripp!' Owen raised his voice.

'Is odd,' Zara agreed, 'but he's nothing to do with me. I am staying here.'

'You are the most infuriatingly stubborn person I know,' Owen's eyes glittered with annoyance. 'Don't you realise you could be in danger?'

'Maybe I am but it's my problem, not yours. By the way,' Zara zipped open her backpack, 'I found this.' She produced a sheet of paper with a flourish.

'What is it?'

'The missing form.'

'Where did you get it?'

'Anthony had it all along. When I realised what it was I stuffed it into my bag. '

'What was Anthony doing with it?'

'Something else I can't explain but the important thing is we have it back.' Zara searched in her bag for a pen. 'Where do

I sign?'

'Wait a moment,' Owen snatched the paper out of her grasp.

'Hey, what are you doing?'

'I don't like this.' Owen scanned the contents.

'What do you mean?'

'This document.'

'You had it drawn up. I'm ready to sign and if you're looking for witnesses I'm sure Stan will oblige.'

'Where did you say you found it?'

'On Anthony's work surface. I disturbed it when I shook out that smelly rug. Hey,' Zara's brow cleared, 'Ned said it was Drosselmeyer's, that's why he was trying to pull if off poor old Anthony.' Her eyes lit up with amusement. 'I must say you weren't very good at controlling him, were you?'

'The dog was in a highly excitable state.'

'He probably wanted revenge for that stone you threw at him.' Zara paused. 'You know one thing still puzzles me.'

'Just the one?' Owen asked in a deceptively mild voice.

'Why did Anthony and Mertice go to all the trouble of making undercover visits to each other? If they wanted to keep their marriage a secret why didn't they live together as man and wife?

'It's not as if anyone minds these days. There was no need to make such a mystery of things.' Zara hit her forehead with the palm of her hand.

'Of course, Anthony's beliefs would have prohibited it, but that would mean their marriage isn't legal, wouldn't it? Duncan's right. There's a story here somewhere.'

'Have you finished?' Owen enquired.

'I think so, yes,' Zara said, 'I'm feeling quite light-hearted now everything's cleared up except for my interview and I'm confidently expecting a green light on that.'

'I hardly think Mertice is likely to divulge the details of her private life to you.'

'Maybe not, but I will have opened the door for Duncan, won't I?'

Owen looked at the paper he was still

clutching.

'Anthony must have taken this on purpose.' He spoke slowly as if he was thinking things through.

'Whatever.' Zara uncapped her pen. 'We have it back, so no more delays.'

'He must have had a reason.' Owen withheld it from her grasp.

'He probably didn't mean to pick it up. Stop looking for more problems. You came to Xena specifically to get me to sign it and that is what I am going to do.'

A shout down in the harbour distracted Owen and Zara grabbed the paper out of his hands and scrawled her signature in the designated box.

'There. Our divorce is finalised.' A lump lodged in the back of Zara's throat.

'It isn't finalised yet.' Owen sounded as though he too had difficulty speaking.

'I'm sure I can leave the tidying up of odds and ends to you. You are now free to catch the next boat home.'

'Then this is goodbye,' Owen said.

'I suppose it is,' Zara agreed, hoping her voice wouldn't give out. 'I wish you and Mossy all the happiness in the world and now if you'll excuse me I need some air.'

Storm Brewing

Standing on the scrap of ground bordering the road outside Stan's taverna Zara took several calming breaths in an effort to control the rapid beating of her heart.

Right now contact with Mertice Yo was out of the question but she needed to do something to take her mind off her divorce.

A crocodile of children skipped past accompanied by two adults. The youngsters were clutching brightly coloured mountain flowers and chattering happily amongst themselves. A brisk walk would provide the perfect outlet to work off the day's stress, Zara decided.

She would follow the small arrows indicating the tourist route favoured by trekkies, day-trippers over from the mainland in search of island scenery.

She shaded her eyes against the strength of the sun, welcoming the discomfort of its relentless heat. She wanted to feel uncomfortable. She needed a physical focus, one that didn't include Owen Jones.

Carpets of wild flowers bordered the rocky path that led up to more challenging territory. Puffball clouds gathered on the horizon as Zara strode on. The angle of the sun heightened and her skin prickled in protest from the heat.

She ignored the discomfort until her hair clinging to the back of her neck in a damp tangled mass became too uncomfortable to ignore. The wind blowing in from the sea offered little relief from the intensity of the sun and forced Zara to the reluctant decision to turn back.

The scudding clouds were threatening to develop into something more serious and she was ill prepared to face one of the dramatic changes in weather for which Xena was renowned.

She looked down at the rock-strewn pathway. The absence of arrows indicated that somewhere along the line she must have strayed off the official route. She turned too quickly and her ankle twisted under her as she trod on some loose stones.

She cried out then limped on for a few more steps before accepting serious progress was out of the question. In the distance she heard the distinct rumble of thunder.

She had no protection against one of the island's violent storms and she knew from experience how quickly they could develop and the devastation they could cause.

Zara stopped to think. She had strayed off the beaten track. Help could be a long time coming. All she could hope for was a lone hiker. A crack of lightning split the darkened sky and an uneasy wind stirred the vegetation.

Perching on a rock Zara eased her injured foot out of its sandal and gently massaged her swollen ankle.

Startled by a movement behind her she swivelled round to confront a wild goat poking its head through some foliage. It bleated before disappearing over the rocks.

'Hello?' Zara called out hoping for an

accompanying human presence. 'Is anyone there?'

The only response was another rumble of thunder.

Tiring of its game, the goat skipped off, leaving an increasingly concerned Zara to take stock of her situation. Stan would be out looking for Ned. Owen had probably taken the water taxi back to the mainland, his mission accomplished. It was a chilling thought to realise there was no-one else on the island to miss her.

Zara tried to block out any negative thoughts but it wasn't easy to think positively with her ankle now swelling up at an alarming rate.

Faint strains of music drifted up from the harbour bars and restaurants. They would be opening up for the evening's entertainment but with the impending storm people would be moving inside and fastening their shutters. There would be no one to hear her cries for help.

A cynical smile twisted Zara's lips. If nature took the worst possible course her signature on Owen's wretched piece of paper wouldn't be needed after all. She straightened up and shook herself back to her senses. She wasn't going to hang around and let nature get the better of her. Rescue had to be her option. The question was how to go about it.

As if in answer to her question a light flashed in her eyes.

'Who's there?' she called out.

The flashlight danced over her head obstructing her vision. A figure stepped out of the shadows.

'Ned?' She identified his lanky silhouette, 'Ned Tripp?'

'What are you doing out here?' he asked.

'I've twisted my ankle.'

Ned knelt down beside her. With surprising gentleness he inspected her injury.

'Didn't anyone tell you it's not wise to wear sandals up here?'

A fat blob of rain landed on Zara's arm.

'Can we save the lecture until later? In case you hadn't noticed there's a storm brewing.'

Ned inspected the darkening sky.

'Lean on me,' he instructed.

Zara tried to put weight on her ankle then collapsed against him.

'I don't think I can go far.'

'You don't have to. I hang out in one of the caves.'

'Did you know,' Zara gasped, 'everyone's down in the harbour looking for you?'

'Don't talk.' Ned tightened his grip around her waist.

Pounding rain was making the ground slippery and it was difficult to gain a foothold. The grains of black earth under their feet were as sharp as shards of glass and progress was slow.

More than once Zara fell against Ned but he possessed a wiry strength and didn't flinch against the pressure of her body weight.

The rain was now so heavy it was difficult to see where they were going.

'Is it much further?' She could feel her legs weakening under the strain.

Ned indicated a small bush bowed low from the relentless rain.

'We've arrived.' He pulled back the dripping greenery to reveal a basic campsite nestling under some sheltering rocks. 'See, it's dry and warm. Let's get you inside.'

He eased Zara down on to a camp bed and placed a rough pillow under her back.

'Rest up while I see to things.'

Zara closed her eyes in relief.

'Don't faint on me.' There was a note of panic in Ned's voice as he passed her a towel. 'My skills don't run to mouth to mouth resuscitation.'

'I don't do fainting,' Zara responded still battling with her breath.

A rare smile lit up Ned's face.

'I'm pleased to hear it.' He produced a damp compress. 'Wrap this round your ankle. I'm afraid it's going to be very painful in the morning.'

The throbbing eased as Zara applied the compress.

'Do you mind if I do another quick

inspection?' Ned asked. 'To check for broken bones.'

'I'm fine.'

Zara towel dried her hair and eased away from him. So far he had played the part of rescuer to perfection but there were too many gaps in his background for her to feel totally comfortable in a one to one situation.

'You shouldn't be up here without adequate supplies.' He was frowning again. 'Are you warm enough?'

Zara nodded. Her teeth were beginning to chatter and she didn't trust herself to reply.

'I'll get a fire going. I would lend you my jacket but it seems to have disappeared.'

'It was dragged out of the harbour earlier today.'

'Was it?'

'That's why everyone is looking for you. The locals think you might have jumped in.'

'I can't swim.'

'They don't know that.'

'Some youths have discovered my hideout and often raid my camp. No-one knows what I'm doing here so they make my life as uncomfortable as possible. They probably thought stealing my jacket was a fun thing to do.'

'What are you doing here?' Zara asked against a background of rain pounding the hillside and overhead thunder almost making speech impossible.

'It's a long story,' Ned replied.

'I think it will be a while before we go anywhere,' Zara encouraged him.

Ned Tripp looked younger in the unusual comfort of his camp and Zara started to relax.

'Hang on while I get my fire going,' he said.

Gentle flames flickered softening the harshness of their surroundings as Ned added foliage and twigs to the blaze. He sat back against a convenient rock and stared thoughtfully into the depths of his fire.

'Something happened to me a while ago before I came to the island.'

'I'm listening.'

'Drink this.' Ned filled a mug with hot tea.

Zara sipped the scalding liquid.

'Where did you learn to make such good tea?'

'When you've been in the army you learn to live off the land.'

'Tea bags and sugar,' Zara took another sip. 'Grow on trees, do they?'

Ned's smile changed his expression from earnest schoolboy to someone caught in the act of telling a fib.

'I have to admit those supplies came from the village shop. I've also got bread, cheese and olives and cinnamon doughnuts. Have one.'

The warmth of the tea started to thaw Zara's chilled bones.

'What happened to you before you came to the island?' she persisted as she bit into a doughnut.

Ned swirled his tea round in his mug. Picking up a spoon he stirred it and drank the contents before replacing his mug on the ground.

'I found out about my father.' His voice sounded controlled as though he were struggling not to let his emotions get the better of him.

'Would you care to go back to the beginning?' Zara licked icing sugar off her fingers.

'Explanations could take some time.'

Ned remained silent for so long Zara thought he wasn't going to say any more.

'Have I touched a raw nerve?' she prompted in a gentle voice. 'You don't have to continue if you don't want to.'

'It was painful at first,' Ned shifted position slightly, 'but after I'd got over the initial shock I knew I had to do something.'

'And?' Zara urged hoping his explanation would eventually make sense.

'The first thing I needed to do was to speak to Mertice but she won't see me.'

'She doesn't see anyone apart from Father Anthony.'

'You're here for media purposes, aren't you?'

Zara stiffened at the note of censure

in his voice.

'You don't approve?'

'I don't approve of people making money out of another's misery.'

'That's pretty strong language.'

'What happened wasn't pretty.'

'Is this anything to do with Iannis Theodorous?' Zara's curiosity was piqued as she began to follow his thread.

'You know about him?' Behind his spectacles Ned's eyes bore into hers.

'Who doesn't?'

'There are people out there still affected by his get-rich-quick scheme.'

'And your father was one of them?'

'You look cold.' Ned unearthed a blanket. 'Wrap this around your shoulders. It could be a long night.'

'I can't stay here all night,' Zara protested.

'You have no choice.'

'I do.'

'You can't escape.' The tone of Ned's reply froze Zara to the spot. Unable to say anything she looked at him in dumb horror. 'I've laced your tea.'

As he spoke Zara's head fell forward and the mug she was holding slipped from her fingers and shattered as it fell to the ground.

'Something's wrong.' Owen and Conrad sat opposite each other on Stan's terrace.

'What sort of wrong?' Conrad's eyebrows met his shaggy fringe.

Owen hesitated as if reluctant to reply.

'Forgive the personal question,' Conrad continued, 'but is it between you and Zara?'

Owen nodded.

'Demi suspected something of the sort the night you stayed over.'

'Your wife's a smart lady,' Owen acknowledged.

'She sensed tension?' Conrad raised his voice at the end of his question.

'We have issues — yes.'

'Demi is no fool. You spent the night out on the balcony, didn't you?'

'Was it that obvious?'

'Like I said — nothing gets past Demi.'

'Zara and I tried to disguise our differences but I suppose we're not very good actors.'

'Want to offload? I know I have a big mouth but you can trust me. I'd never go public on a friend.'

'Zara and I had words,' Owen admitted.

'It happens to us all, but there's more, isn't there?'

'She walked out on me hours ago. I hung around because I didn't want to leave things as they were but she hasn't come back.'

'Tricky.' Conrad frowned.

'Zara's fiery. We'd both be the first to admit it but she's not one to hold a grudge.'

'If she hasn't come back she must be real upset. What did you say to her?'

Owen shook his head.

'I can't tell you.'

'Private stuff?' Conrad queried before continuing. 'My advice for what it's worth is you guys should get your act together. Believe me, I speak from experience.

'Things were bad for a long while between me and my first wife Jodie until we realised griping at each other wasn't the answer but the truth didn't hit us until we sat down and had it out.'

'I think we're past that stage.' Conrad listened intently the expression on his face giving nothing away as Owen continued. 'I want to make sure Zara's OK. Good enough for you?'

'Before we go anywhere with this,' Conrad insisted, 'you have to fill in some gaps.'

'There isn't time.'

'There's always time for a friend.'

'Don't you need to get back to Demi?'

'Heck no, when she and her cousin Melina get together there's no stopping them. I'm better off out of it. So quit stalling and tell me all.'

When Owen finished his edited narrative of recent happenings Conrad leaned back his eyes wide with surprise.

'A quick recap here — Father Anthony's in hospital, you've met Mertice Yo and you and Zara are having a hiccup in your relationship. Did I miss anything out?'

Owen hesitated reluctant to admit he and Zara were effectively divorced and he was engaged to another woman.

'There's a loner hanging around called Ned Tripp.'

'The guy they're out looking for?'

'His jacket was fished out of the harbour.'

'Did you say Ned Tripp?' Conrad sat up straight.

'I forgot to mention him earlier.'

'Owen, he is crucial to the plot.'

'What plot?'

'Don't you know who he is?'

'I thought he might be stalking Mertice.'

'If he's who I think he is he's on a totally different agenda.'

'You know him?'

'I know of him. Look, before we get down to business why don't you check Zara hasn't come back and gone up to her room without you knowing?'

'I'm not sure she'd answer the door.'

'You must have had one heck of a disagreement.'

Owen lowered his eyes to the table.

'I think it's possible she's been kidnapped.'

'What?' Conrad knocked the table leg with his knee, spilling their drinks.

'I'm serious.'

'Brother, you are delving into the realms of fantasy. Why would Ned Tripp want to kidnap Zara?'

'I didn't say I suspected Ned Tripp,' Owen's mouth was set in a grim line, 'but you're right. He is my prime suspect. Tell me what you know about him.'

'If I've got the right Ned Tripp and you have to admit it's an unusual name, his father David Tripp was in cahoots with Iannis Theodorous.'

'Was?'

'Hear me out.' Conrad raised a hand to stall Owen. 'David and Iannis were business partners and like I said, it was fortunate Iannis died when he did. From stories I've heard there wasn't much of a paper trail and apart from rumours about David Tripp creaming off most of the money it was difficult to prove what happened. Then David Tripp also died and that left a lot of people unhappy, as you can imagine. Without his input the investigation virtually ceased.'

'Was Mertice involved in the scam?'

'She was Iannis's constant companion.' Conrad shrugged. 'Who's to say what part she played?'

'Why would David's son want to get in touch with her?'

'She inherited Iannis's property portfolio and we don't know what else.'

'Then she could hold the key to the whole affair.'

'Perhaps without knowing it, but why would you think Ned would want to kidnap Zara? She's nothing to do with Iannis or Mertice.'

'She could be Ned's bargaining tool,' Owen reasoned. 'Mertice wouldn't like to be involved in a kidnapping even if she had nothing to do with it.'

'Sounds far-fetched to me. Besides, didn't you say Ned's jacket was fished out of the harbour?'

'Earlier today.'

'You don't think it's more likely he came to terms with the fact that his was a lost cause and that he might have taken the easy way out? You know — unable to face the family shame?'

'If you mean do I think he jumped, my answer is no.'

'Why?'

'He didn't strike me as a quitter.'

'You never know what people will do under pressure.'

'You're right there. You should have seen the way Father Anthony reacted that day we were all having a picnic together. I'm sure he knew who Ned Tripp was. He changed from being a genial host to a monster in a matter of moments.'

'I'm not into psychology but it suggests to me the two guys have history.'

'I'm convinced Father Anthony knows something he's not telling us.'

'Demi says there are rumours Mertice and Father Anthony are more than good friends and that the religious bit is no more than a cover.'

'They're married,' Owen replied.

'Any more surprises?' Conrad demanded, 'And can you be certain of your facts?'

'It's true all right. Mertice told us herself and I don't care whether they're married or not, I want Zara back.'

'Sure you do.' Conrad attempted to calm Owen down.

'She wouldn't listen to reason. I told her she was delving into dangerous territory and she should leave well alone. That's why I'm convinced something's happened to her — and have you seen the weather?' Owen gestured across the harbour to where the last of the thunder was rumbling away. 'If she's out in this storm . . .'

'Take it easy, we'll find her. She's a feisty lady and I'm sure she'll hold her quarter so no worries there.'

'Where can she be?' Owen gulped down the last of his drink then looked at his glass as if he couldn't understand what it was doing in his hand.

'I guess Stan doesn't know where she is?'

'He's out looking for Ned Tripp.'

'This disappearance thing is getting to be a habit.' Conrad pulled a face.

'I can't sit here and do nothing.' Owen stood up and paced the length of the terrace.

'Word of advice, Owen,' Conrad cautioned, 'don't do anything foolish.'

'I'm going to pay Mertice a visit. I'm convinced she's the key to all this.'

'I'd sure like to come with you but I should be getting over to Melina's.' Conrad glanced regretfully at his watch. 'If I'm any longer they'll think I'm staying away on purpose.' He squeezed Owen's arm. 'Keep in touch and if anything, and I mean anything, happens, you know how to contact me.'

* * *

Ghostly shadows loomed out of the darkness and Owen was glad he had thought to bring a torch with him and to wear a gilet over his shirt. The night air was cool after the storm, and for the first time since coming to Xena he felt cold.

Anthony's house was in darkness, much as Owen would have expected. After a quick inspection of the premises he paused to think.

Maybe Conrad was right and he should leave well alone. What he was doing wasn't fair to Mossy. The sensible thing would be to catch the first water taxi to the mainland. Zara had made it clear he was no longer a part of her life. His future was with Mossy.

Headlights arced through the approaching dusk as he pondered what to do.

'Which way have you come?' Owen flagged down the driver.

'From the hospital,' the driver replied.

'You didn't pass anyone on the road?'

The driver shook his head.

'We saw no-one. It's not the night to be out.' He glanced in the rear view mirror to where his passenger was sitting behind him. 'Madame Yo, did you see anything?'

She frowned at Owen as if she didn't

recognise him.

'How is Father Anthony?' Owen asked. 'You remember Zara and I discovered him on the floor of his kitchen?'

'Of course.' Mertice acknowledged his explanation with an incline of her head. 'Thank you for your concern. I hope he will return home tomorrow. He had forgotten to take his medication and he fainted and banged his head. Thank you for all you did. Who were you looking for?' she added.

'Zara, my wife,' Owen said.

'You are the couple who spent your honeymoon on Xena, aren't you? I'm glad you came back. Come and see me tomorrow.

'Now please, driver, perhaps we could continue our journey? I have had a tiring day and I need some rest.'

The car swept past Owen leaving him in darkness, with the stark realisation he was no further forward with his enquiries into Zara's disappearance than he had been an hour ago.

Desperate Search

'Right, updates.' Conrad strode into the breakfast bar the next morning and grabbed an uneaten croissant off Owen's breakfast tray. 'You promised to keep me in the loop, remember?'

Owen looked up from the map he was studying.

'I have a date with Mertice later today.'

'You saw her?'

'I did and she invited me up to hers.'

Conrad drew out a chair and sat down opposite Owen.

'And?'

'She hadn't seen Zara on the road from the hospital.'

'What's with the map?'

'I'm trying to work out where Zara could have gone.'

'She's still not back?'

Owen shook his head.

'Then we do have a problem,' Conrad snapped to attention. 'What about Ned?'

'No-one's seen him either.'

'If you think he's holding Zara prisoner you don't need maps — you have to get out there and find her, not hang around in the bar of the local taverna. What's got into you? Have you contacted the police?'

'Hey,' Demi appeared in the doorway, 'you're not trading shares across the floor now, Conrad; stop shouting at Owen.'

'Sorry, hon.' Conrad gave a shamefaced smile. 'Owen's told me Zara still hasn't come back. She's been out all night.'

'That is serious.' Demi advanced into the room.

'I don't want to involve the authorities,' Owen said.

'Why not?' Demi asked.

'If I'm wrong and it's nothing to do with Ned it's unfair to come down on him or Mertice.'

Demi opened her mouth to speak but Conrad got in first.

'Two hours — then you can forget your finer feelings! We call in the police. Deal?'

Owen hesitated then nodded.

'Deal,' he agreed.

'Right — action stations!' Conrad swallowed the last of his croissant.

'I need to put the word out to my cousin,' Demi announced. 'Try not to worry, Owen. It's not a big island and my family knows most of its secrets. We'll find her. Do you have any idea in which direction she headed?'

Owen shook his head.

'Conrad told me Zara was wearing light clothes and sandals?' Demi looked thoughtful.

'Yes.'

'Not suitable attire for trekking. She cannot have meant to go far.'

'Have you tried texting her?' Conrad demanded.

'Stan found her mobile on the bar. She didn't take it with her.'

'You know for a sensible girl she can sure act dumb at times.'

'Conrad, you are being impolite. Zara is Owen's wife.

'I suggest we get up a party and take

one of the less challenging walks up to the hills. They are popular with people who don't want to trek but would like to take in the scenery.

'If Zara was,' Demi paused, 'upset, she may have wanted some time alone. Leave it to me. I will organise local help.'

Demi hurried off.

'Tell me it's none of my business,' Conrad began. 'But . . . the quarrel?'

Owen sighed.

'You may as well know, Zara and I are getting divorced and yesterday she signed the final paper.'

'Gee, that's real sad. No going back?'

'The truth is I am engaged to someone else.'

Conrad's greeny blue eyes reflected his surprise.

'No wonder Zara took to the hills. Perhaps you should be getting back to the mainland and your fiancée and leave the search party to us?'

'No way. It's my fault Zara took off. I have to find her. Mossy will understand.'

'Whatever you say,' Conrad acknowledged. 'Let's get the show on the road.'

With one or two locals rounded up by Demi and a handful of student volunteers the search party set out. Soon everyone was breathing heavily from the heat of the morning sun and Demi passed round bottled water while they took a breather.

'Zara would, I think, have found the walk heavy going,' Demi said. 'I am struggling and I am more used to the climate than she would be.'

'Perhaps we should rest up a little longer?' Conrad eyed the students with concern. Several of them were flagging.

'If it's all right with you I'm pressing on.' Owen gripped the stout stick he had been using as support.

'What's that?' One of the female students bent down, spying a shiny object on the ground.

'Here, use my stick,' Owen offered.

Looping it through the buckle she lifted it up and studied it.

'It looks like it's come off a sandal,'

she said.

'Owen snatched it from her fingers.

'It's Zara's.'

'Are you sure?' Conrad demanded.

'As sure as I can be; one of the straps on her sandal was loose.'

'The ground bears evidence of an incident, perhaps a fall.' A guide was inspecting the surrounding area. 'The wooden handrail is broken and the vegetation is flattened in places. There has been a disturbance of some sort. There are animal tracks, too.'

'You mean she has been attacked?' A fearful look crossed one of the student's faces.

'Hush up.' Another student raised his hand and called for silence.

'What is it?' Demi asked.

Silence fell on the small group as they strained their ears.

'It sounds like rustling.'

The female student looked nervously over her shoulder and moved closer in to her companions.

'Are wild goats dangerous?' she asked

in a fearful voice.

'It's coming from over there.' Owen pointed to the wooded area behind them.

'Here is a good place to shelter,' the guide acknowledged. 'There are many secret places well hidden from view. The trees provide natural cover. Maybe your friend has taken refuge up there.'

'Ease up.' Conrad panted behind Owen as he strode off in the direction of a clump of cypresses. 'We're not all as match ready as you.'

The guide parted a mauve clump of spiky flowers to reveal a hidden alcove.

'Go away,' a voice bellowed out of nowhere.

'Hey,' Conrad stumbled as he lost his footing, 'who goes there?'

'Please,' Demi implored, 'be careful, we do not want any more accidents.'

'We're looking for Zara Lennox, the English lady.' Owen cupped his hands. 'Show yourself.'

A tousled head appeared from behind the foliage and blinked nervously at them.

'Ned?'

'Steady,' Conrad cautioned as Owen clenched his fist.

'If he's got Zara . . .' he said through gritted teeth.

'Give the guy a chance, why don't you?'

'Zara's with me. She fell. I rescued her,' Ned garbled an explanation. 'She can't walk and I couldn't leave her and it was raining.'

'Where is she?' Owen moved in, a menacing look on his face, 'What have you done with her?'

'Nothing.' A groggy Zara emerged from behind Ned. There were dark circles under her eyes and a large bruise on her forehead. Ned placed a protective arm around her and she clung on to him for support.

'Get your hands off her,' Owen ordered.

'Stay where you are, Ned,' Zara pleaded, 'I'll fall down if you don't.'

'Why didn't you contact us?' Owen demanded.

'How were we supposed to do that? Smoke signals?' Zara glared at Owen.

'This is my property.' Ned, who was still supporting Zara, made gestures at them.

'The mountains belong to everyone,' their guide shouted before frowning at him, 'Are you the person who lost his coat in the harbour?'

'So what if I am?'

'Patrols have been out looking for you. You have wasted many people's time.'

'It wasn't my fault. Someone stole my coat. You ought to police the area better. I've had no end of things taken.'

'This is getting us nowhere. I'm going in,' Owen announced and bounding forward attempted to wrench Zara away from Ned.

'I don't need your help.' She wriggled away from him.

'Yes, you do,' Owen insisted.

'Give the lady some space.' Conrad gestured to the students to back off.

'Your ankle looks about ten times its normal size.' Owen was still glaring at Zara.

'Ned put some stuff on it.'

'There's no stuff in the world to cure that in a hurry.'

'Thanks for all your help, guys,' Conrad addressed the open mouthed students who were following the exchange agog with curiosity, 'we can take it from here.'

'If ever you are in Xylon,' Demi attempted to sweeten the mood, 'you must come and visit us. Our door is always open.'

'If you're sure the lady doesn't need any help?' The student leader cast a wary glance in Owen's direction.

'She's fine.' Owen added belated thanks to those of Conrad's. 'Enjoy the rest of your day.'

The students shuffled away.

'I think if we're organised about this,' Conrad took charge of the situation, 'Owen and I can make a cradle and carry Zara down between us. You ankle needs attention, Zara, the sooner the better.'

'You'd better come along too, Ned.' Owen still sounded angry. 'You've got some explaining to do.'

'I was trying to help,' he insisted.

'Explanations can wait, guys.' Conrad forced himself between Zara and Owen. 'Right, Zara, if you'll put one arm round my neck and the other round Owen's we'll get going.'

Surrendering to the inevitable, Zara allowed herself to be manhandled down the rocky path and back to the village.

'Zara.' Stan greeted her with a kiss on both cheeks. 'My poor girl, you have been injured.'

'I twisted my ankle,' she explained as she disentangled her arms from Owen and Conrad's necks.

'My cousin will dress it for you. Here she is.' He introduced an older woman dressed in black who took one look at the injury, tutted loudly and proceeded to wave her arms at everyone else.

'Lucrezie says we must give her room to work,' Stan translated.

'I will stay with her,' Demi insisted, 'Lucrezie does not speak English. Why don't you make yourselves comfortable out on the terrace?'

Following her advice, Conrad, Owen and Ned settled down under a canopy of plane trees. Ned glanced at the other two, an uneasy look on his face.

'If you don't mind, Owen, I'll take the chair,' Conrad insisted.

Owen looked about to object then gave a brief nod.

'Ned,' Conrad addressed him in a no-nonsense voice, 'you owe us an explanation.'

The Story is Out

Before Ned could speak, Stan appeared and deposited a tray of cool drinks on the table.

'The guide has gone to tell everyone to call off the search for Ned,' he said, his eyes alight with curiosity.

'Thank you,' Owen replied. 'If you could make sure no-one disturbs us?' he added. With a reluctant agreement, Stan retreated back to the bar. 'Your father was David Tripp, wasn't he?'

Conrad started his interrogation. 'How did you find out?' Ned asked. 'Your surname was a clue and the fact you are stalking Mertice Yo.'

'I'm not stalking her,' Ned protested. 'I've been trying to see her to say how sorry I was for what happened. Iannis should never have got the blame.'

'David Tripp was the brains behind the sting, wasn't he?' Conrad pursued his line of enquiry.

Ned nodded, an unhappy look on his

face. 'I suspected as much,' Conrad said. 'After my father died I was at a loose end.
I had no friends. People didn't want to know me.
'I've always found social situations difficult and I drifted.'
'Go on,' Owen urged, leaning forward, his eyes fixed on Ned's.
'There came a time when I knew I had to go through his things but I didn't want to. I have no close family so there was no-one else to do it.' Ned drank some of the water Stan had placed in front of him.
'By pure chance I found out about a secret fund.' Ned swallowed nervously. 'There's quite a lot of money in it and it should enable me to reimburse the people affected by my father's get-rich-quick scheme, but I needed Mertice's input.
'I had no idea of the state of my father's affairs and I thought perhaps she could help me, seeing as she was so close to Iannis.'
'Did you know Iannis?' Owen demanded.

'I never met him.'

'Did you know Father Anthony and Mertice are married?'

'I suspected something of the sort,' Ned admitted. 'I saw them visiting each other at night. It wasn't difficult to put two and two together. If they weren't married something was going on.'

'Why didn't you approach the authorities?' Conrad asked.

'I've never got on well with authority.' Ned lowered his gaze. 'I was in the army for a while but it didn't suit me. When we parted company by mutual consent I was at a loose end. I tried various careers but I couldn't settle to anything.'

'You didn't follow your father into finance?'

'Not my scene.' Ned looked horrified at the thought.

'So . . . your father's secret fund,' Owen persisted.

'He had a safe hidden behind a picture in his office. I like figures but I couldn't crack the code. I tried birthdays, memorable dates but nothing worked.

'I was going through his desk one day when I had nothing else to do. One of the drawers fell on to the floor. As I put it back I found a list of numbers hidden taped to the bottom.'

Conrad ran a hand through his hair.

'You're kidding. It's straight out of the plot of a dime novel.'

'Don't knock it.' Ned gave a reluctant smile. 'As a system it works.'

'You can say that again,' Conrad was forced to agree. 'Right, these numbers of yours were the combination to open the safe?'

'It wasn't easy to decipher the correct code because they were all mixed up, but like I said I had nothing else to do. I played around with the numbers and eventually a set I came up with worked.'

'And?' Owen fidgeted in his seat.

'And what?'

'For heaven's sake! What happened next?'

'I found details of an account with a significant amount of money in it. It wasn't in my father's name and it looked as though it had been the victim of creative accounting.

'I didn't know what to do with it so I approached one of my father's former colleagues. From time to time he and I kept in touch with each other. He had left my father and set up on his own.

'He did an audit, ran the results past his legal team and they said everything appeared to be in order and as my father's sole surviving heir the money was mine.'

'At the expense of all the poor investors taken in by your father and Iannis.' Owen's voice was full of disgust.

'Hey,' Conrad cautioned, 'the guy's been trying to put things right here.'

'I'm not a fan of capitalists who get rich at other's people's expense,' Owen retaliated.

'Now you know why I quit the rat race,' Conrad agreed. 'I was in danger of turning into one.' He turned back to Ned.

'Are we talking big ticket numbers here?'

'More than I could understand,'

Ned replied.

'Phew.' Conrad pretended to mop his brow. 'I thought I'd seen it all but you get top grade.'

'I didn't want to benefit from the proceeds of a fraud and that's when I got the idea to give the money back, but I knew my father wasn't popular on the island of Xena so I decided to adopt the disguise of a fan as I didn't think Mertice would want to see the son of the man who had been Iannis's failed business partner.'

'Makes sense to me,' Conrad concluded. 'Owen?'

'I suppose it fits.'

'Then things started happening.' Ned was speaking again. 'Zara arrived and began making a nuisance of herself.'

'She's good at that,' Owen agreed.

In the background he could hear Lucrezie conducting a running commentary on the state of Zara's ankle and what he suspected was a tirade against foolhardy tourists who would insist on trekking without the proper equipment.

Catching his eye, Demi cast Owen a

raised eyebrows smile.

'I wanted to get to Mertice before anyone else in authority spoke to her. I didn't know how to go about it and I didn't have much success.

'After Father Anthony had his attack I decided it was too much for me to take on and I'd better leave the island. People might have started suspecting I had attacked him.

'I was getting nowhere with my enquiries and the locals resented my presence. My camp was always being broken into by youths and I was running out of cash.'

'You mean you didn't profit from your father's good fortune?' Owen sounded sceptical.

'I haven't touched a penny of it.'

'What happened between you and Zara?' Owen asked again glanced towards where Lucrezie appeared to be finishing up.

The colour was back in Zara's cheeks and she was sporting a huge bandage on her ankle and from Lucrezie's gestures it looked as though she was being instructed not to put weight on it.

'At first I thought Zara had discovered my lair so I hid. When I heard her shriek I realised something was wrong.'

'Why didn't you go for help?' Owen sounded unconvinced by Ned's explanation.

'I doubt anyone would have believed my story and from what you say they would probably have been annoyed to find I wasn't floating in the harbour along with my jacket which incidentally was how I came to lose my mobile phone. It was in the pocket.'

'You could still have taken the chance.'

'Zara needed urgent attention and I didn't want to leave her alone in the middle of a storm so I gave her some tablets to ease the pain and made her as comfortable as I could.

'I decided to wait for first light before deciding what to do. Zara was still asleep when your search party blundered on the scene.'

'You know what, Ned?' Conrad raised his palm. 'You are one of the good guys.'

Ned Tripp hesitated as if unsure how to react then he slapped his palm against Conrad's, his rare smile lighting up his face.

'I did the right thing?'

'Absolutely,' Conrad replied. 'And I think we should help you get your interview with Mertice.'

'You could do that?' Ned's eyes shone behind his spectacles.

'We do have an appointment with her don't we, Owen?' Conrad glanced at his watch. 'I know we're a tad late but no-one seems to worry too much about timekeeping around this neck of the woods.'

'OK, but I need to speak to Zara first,' Owen insisted.

'I'm good with that,' Conrad replied. 'What say we all meet up outside in five?'

Demi made a discreet exit as Owen sat down opposite Zara, his eyes penetrating hers.

'All right, I'll go first, I'm sorry,' she mumbled.

'Do you need a hospital check-up?'

'Lucrezie's done a good job.' Zara pointed to her bandage. 'She isn't as fierce as she looks, you know. She's gone in search of a crutch.

'Apparently her son fell off his motorbike or something and broke his leg. He doesn't need the crutch any more so I can have it. Are you listening?' Zara demanded.

Owen stared blankly back at her.

'If you're figuring out how to tell me what you think of foolhardy females who go walking in flimsy footwear you can forget it. I've already had a lecture from Lucrezie.

'I couldn't understand a word she was saying but I got the general idea.'

'I am plucking up the courage to tell you I have a date with Mertice,' Owen replied.

'Not without me you don't,' Zara protested. 'And how did you manage that?'

'I bumped into her last night when I was out looking for you and she invited me up there today.'

'You were looking for me?' Zara asked

in a faint voice.

'Yes.'

'In the storm?'

'It had passed over.'

'I've caused all sorts of trouble, haven't I?' Zara's eyes were full of remorse.

'That's the reason why I'm going to see Mertice without you.'

'You cannot leave me out of this,' Zara protested. 'It's my shout.'

'I think you'll find we can.'

'No way,' Zara insisted. 'I'm coming with you.'

'You'll slow us down.'

'Us?'

'Conrad, Ned and myself.'

'Ned's going with you?'

'He's David Tripp's son, David was Iannis's partner.'

'Shouldn't he be under arrest or something?'

'There isn't time to tell you about it now but Conrad thinks he's found a solution to the problem.'

'I don't know what's going on but I'm not letting you see Mertice without me.

Lucrezie, *efcharistó*,' Zara accepted the crutch with a beaming smile.

'*Parakaló*.' Lucrezie's wrinkled face moved into the semblance of a smile before she started off on another round of warnings.

'I think she's delivering a re-run of her lecture,' Zara confided to Owen.

'There you are, Owen.' Demi reappeared, 'Conrad and Ned are waiting. Stan and I will look after Zara for you.'

'No need,' Zara struggled to her feet, provoking another outrage from Lucrezie who looked as though she might re-possess the crutch, 'I'm going with them.'

'Be sensible,' Owen tried reasoning with her.

'When have I ever been that?' she demanded.

'Not in a long time.' Owen raised his eyes.

Demi smiled at the pair of them.

'I suppose when Conrad and I have been married as long as you we will quarrel like this. Come along, Lucrezie, let's see if your cousin will taxi my friends up to Madame Yo's.'

'How many cousins does Demi have?' Zara demanded as Demi led a still protesting Lucrezie away.

'No idea.' Owen paused. 'By the way, I told Conrad we are getting divorced.'

'Then shouldn't you be taking your piece of paper back to the mainland to get it filed or whatever it is you want to do with it?'

'I'm sorry if signing it upset you,' Owen spoke slowly his eyes fixed on Zara's, 'I will deal with it in time but for the moment we have other priorities.'

Zara blinked at him.

If she were in Mossy's shoes she would have been on the first flight out here to see what was going on in Xena but then Zara recalled Mossy was in Africa with Sir Robert.

A crowd of curious villagers was waiting outside the taverna as the battered taxi drew up and the driver got out. Word had got round.

The strange person camping in the hills wasn't dead and the English lady had a huge bandage on her ankle and everyone wanted to know what was going on.

Demi greeted the driver with a kiss on both cheeks before breaking into a stream of instructions that earned a tolerant response from the man who was clearly impatient to be on his way.

With Conrad sitting in the front seat and Ned and Owen squashed in the back with Zara, her leg resting on Owen's knees, the driver gunned the engine into life.

A round of applause broke out among the onlookers as they moved forward and feeling like royalty Zara smiled and waved before they set off to keep their appointment with Mertice.

Back in his Arms

Zara clutched the door handle as the taxi negotiated another hairpin bend at breakneck speed. Owen's arm was warm and firm under her touch as she clung on to it with her free hand.

'Does anyone speak the language?' Ned's glasses slipped down his nose as he grabbed the back of the seat in front of him.

'I'll have a go,' Conrad volunteered. 'If you promise to stop pulling my seat out of its fittings.'

Ned relaxed his hold and leaning in Conrad addressed the driver in his native tongue. The driver nodded vigorously and put his foot down harder on the accelerator.

'What on earth did you say to him?' Owen demanded.

'I thought I asked him to slow down.'

'Well, it doesn't seem to have worked.'

'Want me to have another go?'

'Leave it,' Ned implored. 'I get car sick.'

'Now he tells us,' Conrad raised his hands in a gesture of despair.

'Is it much further?' Ned turned pale.

Leaving Conrad and Ned engaged in a heated discussion regarding travel sickness Owen turned back to Zara.

'How are you feeling?'

Zara bit her lip. No way was she going to admit each bump of the boneshaker taxi caused her ankle to throb more than she could have imagined.

'I'm fine.'

'Not far now,' he commiserated.

'Don't worry about me. I can do this.' Zara summoned up a brave smile.

'I didn't doubt it for a moment.' Owen looked as if he were about to say something more before Conrad butted in.

'If everyone could manage to hold on for about five minutes we should be there.'

'Let's hope the journey hasn't been a waste of time and Mertice is in the mood for visitors.' Owen didn't look convinced.

'You said she invited you,' Zara pointed out.

'She doesn't have a very good track record when it comes to visitors and when she realises Ned is with us.' Owen lowered his voice but Ned and Conrad were again trying to persuade the driver to ease up. 'She may refuse to see us.'

'Why is Ned with us?'

'He's David Tripp's son.'

'I know that.'

'He's found some of the missing money in a secret account and he wants to talk to Mertice to see if she can help him track down Iannis's contacts.'

'Why?'

'He wants to make good on their loss.'

'That is brilliant news.' Zara eased her ankle into a slightly more comfortable position. 'Do you think Mertice can help?'

Owen shrugged.

'It depends on what sort of records Iannis left. Financial affairs can be notoriously complex but Conrad thinks it's a viable option and that's why he's come along for the ride.

'He can better explain the details of

Ned's offer. It's more in his line of business.'

'It should be a challenging interview.'

Owen ran a distracted finger down Zara's arm. His touch sent shivers down her spine.

'This is as far as we go,' Conrad announced, as the taxi screeched to a halt.

Everyone lurched forward and there was a warm draught of air as Ned flung open the rear passenger door and almost fell onto the road.

Demi's cousin beamed at them all and tapped his watch as if expecting praise for having completed the journey in record time.

Zara shunted off the back seat and Owen scrambled out behind her. The little group clustered round each other gathering their scattered wits as a mountain goat eyed them up from behind a large rock.

'Keep him away from me.' Zara hopped backwards. 'He looks like my friend from yesterday. He might have designs on my other ankle and I'm not in the mood for games.'

Refusing payment for the trip, the driver turned and was halfway back down the hill before any of them had time to thank him properly.

'It's as well he didn't want any fare,' Conrad remarked wryly. 'After the journey we've just suffered I'd probably have refused to part with a cent.'

'Everywhere looks locked up.' Ned, now recovered from the car journey, strolled over to the iron railings and shook them in the vain hope they might yield to his touch.

'I could climb over,' Conrad volunteered, 'if someone bunks me up.'

'There's a dog,' Ned cautioned. 'A huge great hound.'

'Care to take my place?' Conrad smiled at him.

'I've already met Drosselmeyer.'

'Drosselmeyer?'

'It comes from 'The Nutcracker',' Zara said. 'It's a ballet.'

'I know it's a ballet.' Conrad looked as

though he wasn't listening.

'Drosselmeyer is the godfather. He wears a cloak of stars and a big hat.'

'Well, thanks for that.' He dismissed Zara's explanation with a wave of his hand. 'Tell you what, Ned, let's go over the top together and leave Owen to look after Zara.'

'I'm not good with heights.'

'Any other phobias you forgot to tell us about?' Conrad demanded. 'You don't have issues with iron railings, do you?'

Leading a protesting Ned away, Owen and Zara perched on adjacent outcrops of rock. The sun beat down mercilessly on their backs and Zara realised yet again she was inappropriately dressed for mountain life.

'What do we talk about while we're waiting?' Owen stretched out his long legs in front of him.

'Joanna Moore?' Zara suggested, feeling the need to distance her emotions from Owen and knowing the mention of her old friend's name should be enough to do it.

Owen took a deep breath.

'What do you want to know about her?' he asked in a voice full of reluctance.

'What threw you together?'

'Nothing.'

'That's not an explanation.'

'There never was anything between us so nothing threw us together.'

'Why should I believe you?'

'No reason in the world. She's your best friend. Of course you would believe her instead of me. That's why I didn't say a word against her. You chose to believe her. I was out in the cold.'

'You mean it wasn't true?' Zara felt the first stirrings of guilt.

'What does it matter now?' Owen asked with a weary sigh.

'It doesn't, I suppose, but I would like to know.'

'She came on to me. When I rebuffed her advances she got her revenge by telling you it was the other way round.'

Zara swallowed the lump rising in her throat.

'Her sister backed her up. They never agreed about anything.'

'Was that what swayed you?'

Zara looked down at the ground.

'I suppose it was, but I should have given you a chance to explain.'

'Yes, you should, but if you want the full facts, Lucy's got a huge student debt. Joanna promised to help her out.'

'She paid off her sister's debt at the expense of our marriage?'

'She made a significant contribution but Lucy had more of a conscience than her sister and confessed everything to me.

'She was sobbing down the telephone for what seemed like hours but it didn't make any difference to us because you weren't taking my calls.' Owen lapsed into silence.

'I'm sorry,' Zara admitted. 'I didn't understand.'

'Again there was no reason why you should. Anyway . . . ' Owen broke off speaking as Zara felt herself slipping off her rock. Her good foot went from under her and shrieking she collapsed into Owen's arms.

Zara stayed where was for a few moments feeling the heat of his rapid heartbeat against hers.

'Owen, I . . . ' She raised her face to his.

The next moment his lips descended on hers and it was as if the years slipped away and she and Owen were still living together as man and wife.

Zara clung on to him, giddy with emotion enjoying the sensation of his arms wrapped around her.

'Ah, I hate to disturb you,' a hesitant voice butted in.

Zara tried to step back but her ankle and Owen wouldn't let her.

'Yes?' Owen enquired, his voice rough with emotion.

'Sorry and all that,' an embarrassed Conrad apologised, 'it's just there's something I think you ought to see if you'll follow me.'

The iron gates swung open and the small group made their way through,

Zara clutching on to Owen with Conrad bringing up the rear.

The trees provided a canopy of coolness as they made slow progress down the drive, the scent of pine helping to clear Zara's confusion.

Owen was engaged to Mossy. No way should she have let him kiss her.

'Where's Ned?' she heard Owen ask Conrad.

'With Mertice.'

'You got to see her?'

'We did.'

'And she's speaking to Ned?'

'Yes.'

'I can't walk any faster.' Zara tried, without success, to draw away from Owen. 'If I'm holding you back, go on ahead. I'll catch up.'

'There's a first.' Owen's wry voice made Zara long to take a swing at him with her crutch.

'We're in this together, guys.' Conrad spoke in his cheerleader voice. 'Onwards and upwards. Go, go, go.'

'You're sounding remarkably upbeat.'

Owen frowned. 'What's to know?'

'Wait and see,' Conrad sounded irritatingly smug, 'but it is good news.'

'We could do with some of that,' Owen replied. 'How's the ankle holding up?' He looked hard at Zara whose lips still felt warm from his touch.

'Good.' She hobbled on, wishing she could go faster.

'It's round here.' Conrad guided them past a marble statue of a Greek hero.

'Can you manage the steps up to the veranda?' Conrad asked Zara.

With Owen and Conrad on either side of her Zara half hopped half jumped up the jutting stone steps.

They turned the last corner and found Mertice nursing a pale-looking Anthony. Ned was sitting in a cane-backed chair surveying the proceedings with a look of bemusement on his face.

'There you are,' Mertice greeted them. 'I'm so glad you could make it. I won't ask what you have done to your ankle, Zara. I may call you Zara?'

Zara nodded.

'We'll save that story for another day. You must call me Mertice,' she added before turning her attention back to Anthony and fussing over him, tucking the blanket tidily over his legs. She poured out some fresh water from the jug on the table at his side.

'You're better?' Zara was pleased to see Anthony appeared to have suffered no lasting damage from his fall.

'Alive and kicking, as you can see,' Anthony replied, 'and I have you to thank for that.'

'I didn't do anything.'

'You found me.'

'Stan was worried about you.'

'It is good to have true friends.' Anthony looked thoughtful. 'I feel a great weight has been lifted off my shoulders,' he added. 'Ned has brought us such good news.'

'Right, introduction time,' Conrad announced.

'We know who everyone is,' Owen pointed out.

'No, you don't. You haven't been

introduced to Iannis Theodorous.'

'What?' Zara's crutch fell to the floor, forcing her to cling on to Owen.

Conrad's smile threatened to split his face.

'You know him better as Father Anthony.'

Bolt from the Blue

'Here, sit down.' Owen guided Zara towards a cane-backed chair while she recovered her breath.

'I will arrange for some refreshment. English people like their tea, don't they?'

The sound of Mertice's stiletto heels on the cool tiles as she went in search of tea punctured the silence that followed Conrad's bolt from the blue.

Zara sank into the cushioned comfort of one of her hostess's chairs. Her ankle throbbed mercilessly and she wasn't sure it would have supported her weight much longer.

'You've gone as white as a sheet.' Conrad looked conscience stricken. 'I should have thought before I blabbed out the big news.'

'I don't think I was ready for that,' Zara admitted.

'I don't think any of us were,' Conrad agreed.

Father Anthony smiled nervously as if

waiting for further reaction from her.

'Would you mind repeating the introduction?' Zara asked Conrad.

'Anthony and Iannis are one and the same person.'

'Did you know about this?' Zara swung round to face Ned.

Ned shook his head, dislodging his glasses, which again had slipped down the bridge of his nose.

'No. This is the first I've heard of it,' Ned looked as though he were in physical pain. 'You have to believe me,' he added.

'I'm not sure I know what to believe.' Zara adjusted her foot into a more comfortable position.

'I'm telling the truth,' Ned insisted.

'You recognised Ned on the day of the picnic, didn't you?' Owen accused Anthony.

'Did you?' Ned looked baffled.

'Ned looks like his father.' Anthony volunteered an explanation. 'That's why I was so abrupt with him.'

'You were rude.' Ned now sounded

angry.

'I apologise for my behaviour. I thought you knew who I was. Your father and I worked closely together.'

'My father and I operated on a different wavelength. I told Zara all about it, didn't I?' He turned to her for support.

'Before you laced my tea.'

'What?' Owen exploded.

'With mild painkillers,' Ned clarified. 'They sent Zara to sleep almost immediately.'

'Leave it, Owen,' Conrad cautioned.

'I have to know what he's been up to with my wife.'

'We'll get round to it later,' Conrad said.

'Owen, I'm good,' Zara assured him. 'And I know what you told me, Ned, but how do I know you were speaking the truth?'

'No-one ever believes me.' Ned looked ready to burst into tears.

A guilty silence fell on the small group.

'Ned?' Conrad encouraged, 'the floor is yours and we are all prepared to listen.'

‘I’m not the one who assumed a false identity.’ Ned sounded close to panic.

‘Steady on.’ Owen attempted to calm him down. ‘No-one’s accusing you of anything.’

‘Zara is.’

‘Why don’t you tell us your story?’ Conrad stalled Zara’s response with a smile of encouragement. ‘Maybe that’ll give us a handle on things.’

Ned looked down at the tiled flooring, a mulish look on his face.

‘We haven’t got all day,’ Owen complained.

For a moment Zara thought Conrad was going to strangle Owen.

‘I was away at school then the army,’ Ned mumbled. ‘I saw little of my father. My mother died when I was young and after that,’ he shrugged, ‘my father and I weren’t close. I’ve told you everything else.’

‘Right.’ Conrad appeared to digest this statement then looked to the others for help. ‘Questions, anyone?’

‘I have a question.’

Mertice, who had returned with a tray of tea, poured everyone a cup, kicked off her shoes and curled her feet up on to her seat, reminding Zara of an elegant elfin. She looked every inch the prima ballerina.

'Why were you stalking me?'

'I wasn't.'

'You certainly gave that impression,' Mertice said in gentle contradiction.

'I thought it was a good cover and you might take pity on me and speak to me but when you didn't I grew tired of playing the part.

'I couldn't think of another reason for my being on the island and I was thinking of leaving.'

'I'm good with that,' Conrad said. 'Anthony?'

Anthony looked round at the sea of curious eyes all fixed on him.

'Yes?'

'It's your turn now.'

'I don't know where to start.' Anthony hesitated.

'How about I nudge you in the right

direction?' Conrad looked unusually belligerent. 'Why don't you tell us why you've been pretending to be dead and how you've evaded justice for so long?

Anthony paled.

'Mr Desoutter,' Mertice's expression matched Conrad's, 'if you are going to threaten my husband I shall insist you leave. He's not well — please remember his health.'

'Sorry, ma'am,' Conrad apologised, 'my tongue runs away with me at times.'

'Would you like me to do the talking?' Owen's voice injected some calm into the situation.

'No,' was Mertice's crisp reply. 'My husband has a right to speak and I would ask you all to have the courtesy to listen to him.' Mertice's dark brown robin eyes surveyed the group. Everyone nodded agreement.

'Off you go, my darling.' She gave her husband an encouraging smile.

'I found it easy to assume the identity of a cleric,' Anthony explained. 'I wanted to take up religious orders when I was young until life got in the way so it was a convenient disguise to adopt.' Anthony's eyelids drooped and he stifled a yawn behind the back of his hand.

'You must not tire yourself, my darling,' Mertice insisted. 'The doctor said too much excitement would not be good for you.'

'This is exactly the sort of excitement I want,' Anthony confessed, 'to clear my name.'

'You'll have a challenge on your hands and it won't be easy.' Conrad still looked serious. 'Sorry, Madame Yo, I don't want to upset your husband but I'm telling it like it is.'

'Mertice, please,' she insisted. 'And may I call you Conrad?' she added with a sweet smile.

'I'd be honoured.' He smiled back at her.

'We understand what you are saying,' Mertice continued. 'Anthony and I have done nothing but talk things over for days. We knew our time was running out but we didn't know what to do. You could be our lifeline.'

'I am a bit out of touch with financial things these days,' Conrad said, 'but I'll help in any way I can.'

'That is most kind of you.' Some colour returned to Anthony's face. 'I can't count the number of sleepless nights I've suffered.'

'I used to take my darling for night time drives around the island,' Mertice confessed. 'We didn't want people to see us together so we went out under cover of darkness.'

'So it was your car I heard in the small hours,' Zara said.

'Probably,' Mertice agreed. 'We were desperate for a change of scenery and we didn't know what to do about our situation.

'We knew things couldn't continue as they were but we couldn't see any way out.'

'You've been lucky to get away with the deception for so long,' Conrad said.

'That's why I assumed the mantle of a recluse. After a while people stopped calling.' She paused to look at Zara. 'All that changed when you arrived on the island.'

'And Ned came calling,' Anthony put in. 'Is it any wonder we were starting to panic?'

'That's all very well,' Owen butted in, 'but there are people out there who will want explanations and they won't hold back, illness or no illness.'

Anthony and Mertice exchanged anxious glances.

'I wasn't completely innocent but neither am I a crook. Your father talked a good game, Ned, and he took me in.'

'Along with all the other investors,' Conrad added.

'I wanted to put things right but I couldn't see how.'

'I can help here.' Ned sounded a lot happier.

'There was all sorts of stuff in my father's safe,' he added. 'I didn't have a chance to go through it but with your agreement I'll get on to it as soon as I can.'

'Please do,' Anthony insisted.

'I have a question,' Zara said.

'I'm sure you have many.' Mertice smiled. 'Please keep them brief. Anthony needs his rest.'

'How did you manage to fake your death and why?'

'That is two questions but in the circumstances I will permit them,' Mertice replied.

Anthony looked thoughtful before he started speaking again.

'Like Ned, I needed to go under cover. I had a brother called Anthony. He was the one who died, not me, so I assumed his identity.'

'And no-one outed you?' Conrad could hardly keep the surprise out of his voice.

'No.' Anthony smiled. 'I had always kept a low profile.

'No-one knows Mertice and I are married and we shut ourselves away from the world as best we could.'

'What about the real Anthony?' Owen asked. 'Surely someone realised you weren't him.'

'He was a year younger than me and when we were boys people used to think we were twins so the deception wasn't difficult.'

'Then I came blundering on the scene,' Zara said.

'You were a major inconvenience,' Mertice acknowledged, 'and your arrival does seem to have set off a chain reaction of events.'

'I don't know the legality of these things.' Conrad shook his head. 'But it's going to have to come out now. What do you intend doing?'

'Isn't it obvious?' Mertice smiled. 'We are going to clear Iannis's name.'

'Right. Well, on that note,' Conrad stood up, 'I wish you the best of luck, Mertice, you too, Anthony. You know where to find me.'

'You're leaving?' Mertice uncurled her legs. Petite as she was, she barely reached Conrad's chest.

'My wife Demi would like to get back to Xylon tonight. She's got another family party to arrange for the weekend. I've never known a gal with so many cousins and her tribe are big on get-togethers so I'd best be going.'

'Perhaps we should leave, too.' Owen also stood up.

'Thank you.' Anthony smiled. 'I am feeling rather tired.'

'You will always be most welcome to call again. I am so grateful you came back to Xena, Zara and Ned.

'Without you I don't know if we would have had the courage to come clean,' Mertice admitted.

'I'll do all I can to help.' Ned sounded much happier as he sprang to his feet.

'Now you know our guilty secrets,' Mertice implored, 'I would ask for the moment that you do not go public on what we have told you.'

'You have our word,' Owen assured her.

'We will contact the authorities in our own time and I promise we will not run away. My husband has always been an honourable man.'

'I didn't doubt it for a moment,' Conrad insisted.

'I will arrange a taxi back for you,' Mertice's face lit up in an impish smile, 'a reputable one who will drive you at a dignified speed.' She held out a hand to them all.

'Please come again, Zara. Anthony told me about your boss's plans to publicise the island, but you can understand my reluctance to take part in anything right now.

'Once everyone realises Iannis is still alive, life will get rather tricky.'

Zara struggled to her feet.

'We won't bother you any more,' she replied. 'It's been lovely meeting you,' she added with genuine pleasure.

'And take care of your ankle.' Mertice frowned at Zara's bandaged foot.

'That is how my dancing came to an end. I landed badly after a tricky fouette and my career was over in an instant.'

Anthony smiled at them from his prone position.

'Forgive me for not getting up. I would

like to join my wife in saying I don't know if I would have been brave enough to reveal my true identity and I am grateful events have been taken out of my hands.

'It is an enormous relief to know I am going to have a chance to put things right.'

With Mertice waving them off, Ned joined Zara, Owen and Conrad as they clambered into another taxi and were slowly driven back to the taverna.

'If I'm quick I should catch the next water taxi to Xylon. Let me know how things go.'

Conrad bade goodbye to Ned.

'Zara,' he kissed her on the cheek, 'good luck with everything.'

'I'll be off as soon as I've dismantled my camp.' Ned pushed his glasses up the bridge of his nose. 'And thank you.'

'For what?' Owen looked puzzled.

'I've always been a drifter, bit of a loner. You've given me a chance to do something worthwhile.

'I'm going to help Anthony –Iannis — whatever we are supposed to call him, to clear his name.'

'Don't forget to tell the fishermen you didn't jump off the harbour wall,' Owen called after him.

With a brief wave of acknowledgement Ned strode off, leaving Zara to face Owen in the solitude of Stan's bar.

'You'd better be on your way, too,' she said.

'What are you going to do?' Owen asked.

'Wait for my ankle to heal then I'll be leaving. I have to update Duncan so if I don't see you again,' she shrugged, 'I hope you and Mossy will be very happy together.'

'Zara,' Owen called after her. 'Wait.'

'Bye,' she said with a bright smile before hobbling off in search of her laptop.

* * *

'Where have you been?' Duncan's image materialised on the screen in front of her. 'I've been trying to get hold of you for hours.'

'Sorry.' Zara settled down on her bed.
'What's that?' Duncan pointed over her shoulder.
'A crutch. I hurt my ankle.'
'What has been going on?'
'You won't believe what's happened.'
Duncan looked distracted as Zara began her report.
'Are you listening to me? Duncan?' she prompted. 'What's wrong?'
'I need to speak to Owen — urgently,' he told her. 'Is he still there?'
'I don't know,' Zara admitted. 'Want me to ring through to his room?'
'Please.'
Owen answered Zara's call on its second ring.
'Duncan wants a word,' she said.
'Now?'
'He says it's urgent.'
'I'll be right over.'
'What's going on?' Zara asked, intrigued by all the subterfuge.
'You'd better answer the door.' Duncan was saved the trouble of replying.
'Come in,' Zara called out and made

her careful way across the room.

'I'll be downstairs if either of you need me.'

She smiled at Duncan and, easing past Owen, made her way out into the corridor.

Here's to the Future

Stan was sorting out menus behind the bar. He poured Zara a glass of fruit juice and passing it over settled down for a chat.

'Demi tells me you went to see Mertice Yo.'

Zara sipped her drink.

'I did.' She nodded, not sure how much of her visit she should reveal.

Stan and Demi's network of cousins stretched far and wide and it wouldn't take long for the news of Anthony's real identity to go global.

The expectant look on Stan's face faded as he realised Zara wasn't going to tell him what had been going on.

'Your boss has been trying to contact you,' he said.

'I know,' Zara replied.

'He wanted to talk to Owen. I wonder why.'

Zara's thoughts were running much along the same lines.

It could be to arrange another trip somewhere, but Zara doubted Duncan would regard that as a personal matter and he had definitely looked ill at ease.

'Demi said to say goodbye and she hopes to see you the next time you return to the island.'

'I'm not sure I will be coming back.' Zara was feeling flat after all the recent excitement.

'Everyone comes back to Xena,' Stan insisted.

'Are you a philosopher?' Zara teased as the telephone rang in the office.

'Excuse me.' He disappeared into the back room to answer it.

'There you are.' Owen sat on the stool beside Zara's and helped himself to some of the iced orange juice.

'You've finished talking to Duncan?'

'I have. He said to say goodbye.'

'Everyone appears to be saying goodbye to me today.'

'I don't have to rush back. We could travel home together. Do you fancy a break? How about Cornwall? I'll clear it with Duncan if you like.'

'What are you talking about?' Zara frowned at him.

'Duncan told me . . . ' Owen was smiling at her as if suggesting a holiday with him was the most natural thing in the world.

'Told you what?' Zara was starting to lose patience. 'You're talking in riddles.'

'Mossy asked him to pass on a message.'

'What message?'

'She has broken off our engagement.'

Zara jerked, spilling some of her orange juice over the bar.

'Not because of me?' She felt sick in the pit of her stomach.

'No, for once this is nothing to do with you.'

'What happened?'

'She and Sir Robert have,' Owen paused, 'found each other' was how Duncan put it.'

'Found each other?'

'Duncan doesn't do sentiment and he had difficulty putting their relationship into words. What he was trying to say was they have fallen in love.'

'You have to go after Mossy and get her to change her mind,' Zara urged.

'Could be difficult.'

'I'm sure you'll find a way.'

'I've never been into breaking up a marriage.'

Zara blinked.

'Whose marriage are you talking about?'

'Mossy's.'

'Mossy isn't getting married. You told me she's called off your engagement.'

'She called it off because she's already married.' Owen paused. 'To Sir Robert.'

Zara swayed and would have slipped off her barstool if Owen hadn't put out a hand to steady her.

'What?' she gasped.

'They are ideally suited if you think about it; same background, childhood friends, similar work ethic.'

'I thought you loved her.'

'I did, I still do, but not as a future wife.' 'What changed your mind?'

Owen stared into the contents of his glass before raising his eyes to Zara's.

'You.'

'I didn't do anything.'

'Maybe not consciously but when I saw you on the day I arrived down in the harbour with your face covered in sugar and your hair windblown and wild and you were angry and calling me all sorts of names because I'd left you open to bigamy or some such rot I realised I'd never fallen out of love with you although I tried hard to convince myself otherwise.'

'No.' Zara shook her head. 'It isn't right.'

'Isn't it?'

'That's not how I remember it.'

'That's a pity.'

'You can't love me.'

'I admit it can be a struggle at times but I lost the fight.' He grinned as Zara's face flamed. 'Do you feel the same about me?' Owen's voice was little more than an urgent whisper.

'After the kiss we shared?'

'I don't know what you're talking about.'

'You can't have forgotten,' Owen chided, 'but to refresh your memory Ned and Conrad had climbed over Mertice's gates and we were sitting outside waiting for them to come back.

'Remember now?'

Zara nodded, her throat threatening to lock up.

'Are you prepared to give our marriage another try?

'I've shredded the sheet of paper you signed. If you don't believe me you can take a look in my wastepaper bin.

'That's what I was doing when you called my room to tell me Duncan wanted to speak to me.'

'What did you do that for?'

'Even if Mossy and Sir Robert hadn't got together I was going to break things off. I've far too much respect for Mossy to lie to her. I couldn't have gone through with our marriage feeling as I do about you.'

Zara gulped down the last of her

orange juice.

'By the way, Demi sussed us out.'

'Demi?'

'Somehow she figured I'd spent the night on the balcony when we were over on Xylon.

'I suppose I didn't make too good a job of mussing up the bed. I'm sure she would be very happy if we got back together again.'

'And Conrad — does he know how you feel?'

'I didn't tell him everything but he said when things weren't going too well with his first wife they talked things through.'

'What happened?'

'They split up.'

'Great advice,' Zara said with a rueful smile.

'They're still friends.'

The throbbing of Zara's ankle intensified, providing a welcome focus for her emotions.

'Why don't you come down to Cornwall?' Owen coaxed in a soft voice. 'We could take it step by step? Build some broken bridges?'

Zara blinked rapidly.

'I have a job to do here,' she insisted stubbornly.

'I don't think Duncan's documentary on Xena will get the green light once the balloon goes up. In fact the best place to be might be as far away from here as possible.'

'We can't desert Anthony and Mertice.'

'They'll manage without us. They've been through a lot together and I'm sure they'll come out on top.'

'You didn't believe me when I said something odd was going on,' Zara insisted stubbornly.

'Why don't you come down to Cornwall and point out all the other things I've got wrong?' Owen suggested. 'You'd enjoy that.'

'No.'

'No?' Owen echoed, looking less sure of himself.

'If I do come down to Cornwall,' Zara spoke slowly, 'I want to watch the sunrise, eat fish fresh from the sea, enjoy cream teas and let the wind blow my hair all over the place.'

'I won't stop you.' Owen's eyes glittered, as he looked into Zara's.

'When I thought you'd been unfaithful my life fell apart. I vowed never to get involved romantically with anyone else ever again and I haven't,' she paused, 'until now.'

'Are you telling me there's someone else? Is it Duncan?'

Zara cheeks reddened.

'I wasn't telling the complete truth about my relationship with Duncan,' she admitted. 'In fact I was lying. Our relationship is purely professional.'

A cool breeze wafted through the terrace doors creating a welcome breath of fresh air.

'I did it to annoy you,' Zara admitted. 'You were so happy with Mossy and I wanted to get back at you.'

'Does that mean you still care for me?' Owen asked, his voice full of hope.

Zara gave in.

She had tried to fight down her feelings for Owen but she knew there never would be anyone else in her life and now he was no longer engaged to Mossy there never would be.

'Why don't we go down to Cornwall and find out?'

'Good idea.' Owen leapt off his stool.

'Where are you going?'

'To stop the water taxi going without us.'

'So soon?'

'No time like the present and I don't want you changing your mind on me.'

'Can we come in now?'

Conrad and Demi poked their heads round the door.

'I thought you'd gone back to Xylon.' Owen glared at them.

'Change of plan.' Conrad didn't look in the least repentant. 'Demi here decided you had a marriage worth saving so if you hadn't sorted things out between you she was going to have a go.

'I told her not to interfere but as usual she took no notice.'

'Look what Stan found in his wine cellar.' Demi produced a bottle of champagne from behind her back. 'Conrad, get some glasses.'

'Coming right up.'

Demi settled down on an adjacent stool.

'I telephoned Stan and he said to come on over immediately so here I am.'

'How much of that did you hear?' Owen asked her.

'Enough.' Demi sorted out the glasses Conrad had deposited on the bar.

'We'll join you in a toast then we'll leave you alone,' she said.

'Here's to the future,' Conrad raised his glass.

'I've told the water taxi to wait.' Stan rushed in to the bar. 'He said no hurry.'

'Was Stan listening behind the door too?' Zara demanded.

'I'm afraid he was.'

'Anyone else?'

'No, well Lucrezie and Melina, and some of the cousins, but they don't speak much English so your secret is safe with us.'

'As soon as you are ready,' Stan

ushered Conrad and Demi out of the bar, 'let me know and I will arrange a send off party.'

Zara turned to Owen to make a protest but before she could speak his lips descended on hers in a kiss that took her breath away.

'Promise me you'll never leave me,' he murmured in her ear.

'I promise,' she said. 'Now kiss me again.'

Other titles in the
Linford Romance Library:

BEYOND HER DREAMS

Gail Richards

England, 1848. Housemaid Alice is taken from the big house she works in to be the only servant to Mrs Younger. The first person she meets is Daniel, whose friendly face she remembers in the dark, lonely days that follow. She dreams of romance but Daniel has a sweetheart — hasn't he? Then Mrs Younger disappears and it's up to Alice to find her. Will Daniel help or is he too interested in someone else?

A SUITABLE COMPANION

Philippa Carey

Earl Barton's daughter's new governess is collected from the stagecoach stop. However, the next morning they discover Clara Thompson is the wrong young lady — she had been expecting to be companion to a Lady Sutton. But Lady Sutton refuses to exchange her for the intended governess! They have to keep Clara on to help them with the tantrum-prone young Lady Mary while they find a replacement governess. However, could it be that the wrong young lady turns out to be the earl's right young lady?

THE SUMMERHOUSE GHOST

Camilla Kelly

Lizzie is thrilled when her theatre company gets the chance to put on an open-air production at a Georgian country house. As soon as she sees the property she's enchanted by it — and by two of the residents: Griffin, and his foster son, Oscar.

But the house has secrets, and something within it starts to threaten the play, Lizzie's new relationships, and her safety. Something in the house wishes her harm . . .

THE DUCHESS OF SYDNEY

Dawn Knox

Convicted of a crime she did not commit, and sentenced to the colonies in Australia, Georgina had lost all hope . . . until she met Francis Brooks, Lieutenant on the transport ship and tasked with protecting her. Would she ever unravel all the secrets that kept them apart, and would she ever be free again — free to be herself, and free to love?

AFTER THE STORM

Sally Hawker

Coffee, cake and cats: these are a few of Lexie Farrington's favourite things. When she walks into the Thistledean Café in Edinburgh, she's delighted to find all three — including a black cat being held by a very grumpy-looking pirate! Of course, Billy McCreadie isn't really a pirate — he just gives talks about them. But he is in desperate need of a cat-sitter. When Lexie steps in, little does she realise that Billy will be the very man to solve a certain puzzle of her own . . .